is th

Steven Jacobi was born in Birmingham
and educated in Cambridge, Edinburgh
and London. He has also worked in
the Far East. He has just completed a thesis
on Angus Wilson. *Going Naked is
the Best Disguise* is his first novel and
he is currently at work on his second.

GOING NAKED
IS THE
BEST DISGUISE

Steven Jacobi

Minerva

A Minerva Paperback
GOING NAKED IS THE BEST DISGUISE

First published in Great Britain 1995
by Martin Secker & Warburg Ltd
This Minerva edition published 1996
by Mandarin Paperbacks
an imprint of Reed International Books Ltd
Michelin House, 81 Fulham Road, London SW3 6RB
and Auckland, Melbourne, Singapore and Toronto

Copyright © 1995 by Steven Jacobi
The author has asserted his moral rights

A CIP catalogue record for this title
is available from the British Library
ISBN 0 7493 9644 X

Printed and bound in Great Britain
by Cox & Wyman Ltd, Reading, Berkshire

For Carol and Max

PART ONE

– I –

The big enemies in our household were the Rolling Stones, Labour politicians and sensitivity. I was sitting on a potty in front of the television watching Mick Jagger and Keith Richards being arrested, when my mother turned round, careless of my tender years, and said in a clipped, efficient voice, 'If you don't smoke by the time you're twenty-one, I'll give you one hundred pounds.' For someone on two shillings a week, that was a lot of money. I accepted, and refused all cigarettes for the next twenty-five years. I won, and my mother paid without complaint. Considerately, she didn't count the incident with my grandfather's pipe, when I had been violently sick all over his grey stone kitchen floor.

The news item about the Rolling Stones had been followed by one on Harold Wilson. He was subjected to a barrage of scornful abuse from my mother, who was standing on the other side of the lounge.

She never sat down. Ever. She was one of those people who had to be moving at all times. Even when she was on the phone she would be simultaneously talking, wiping surfaces, and drinking sherry out of the white mug with a brash 'Hummel Hummel' slogan on it. Sometimes, and with remarkable ingenuity, she managed to polish the phone itself.

Everyone thinks their families are eccentric. Because my father was often 'away on business', 'working late', 'about to pop down to the Jewellery Quarter', we rarely saw him. My mother had more or less absolute control over my life. I accepted as perfectly normal attitudes and behaviour which I would struggle to discard in later years.

My mother told me that when I was born, I had very bad jaundice and was a sickly custard yellow. I was her fourth. The other three had been stillborn. She also maintained that I was very lucky, and owed everything to her. My father was at a football match at the moment of birth. He had played a game himself that morning, and in the afternoon was standing on the terraces in a camel-coloured overcoat when the public address system announced that he might like to make his way to the hospital. Underneath the coat, he was still wearing the navy-blue kit he had been sporting an hour or so earlier.

The football ground was in the middle of Birmingham, and only five minutes' walk from St Anne's Hospital. He ran there at half-time, saw my mother greased with sweat after thirty-six hours of labour, and managed to make it back for the beginning of the second half. Later, he said that I'd looked 'like the back end of a bus . . . bloody horrible'.

Birmingham beat Sheffied United 3–1, so that was all right.

Two days later, my mother decorated the outside of the semi-detached house they had bought. When my father arrived home from work, he held the ladder.

Most of my earliest memories are of my mother. She used to bath me in the kitchen sink and then carry me upstairs to get a pink towel from the airing cupboard. Sometimes my friend Simon used to share the sink with me. I knew he was my friend because Mother told me so. Simon's mother was called 'Aunty Claire', and she was married to Frank. A few years before, she had spilt hot fat from the chip pan on her face.

'Aunty Claire's had some skin taken off her bottom and put on to her face,' Mother told me.

And then, anticipating my response: 'But you must never stare. You must *never* let her see that you know.'

I never would have known if Mother hadn't told me. She often fed me with embarrassing bits of information. She told my father that he would forget his arse if it weren't fixed on so tightly. I'd asked all my friends' mothers whether they had also left theirs lying around. My mother had a mischievous, vicious streak lurking within, too easily seduced from its hiding place.

She cleaned our house every day of the year, which wasn't particularly remarkable except that she often did it with no clothes on. Sometimes, in the depths of a cold winter for instance, she would compromise with an apron, but otherwise the sight of the pink-trimmed Hoover standing in the hallway ready for action was synonymous with Mother's nakedness.

I felt there was something wrong with this procedure. Even when my friends came to play, she would walk brazenly past them, puffing cushions or shining silverware, flaunting her nudity. News obviously travelled quickly, because I was often invited to other people's houses by worried parents who were anxious lest their own children be exposed to Mother's unclothed figure.

She was unrepentant about her actions, and often muttered things like, 'They're just jealous because they haven't got anything to show off', or, 'I don't see why I should be hindered from doing my work by those stuffy old birds. We're all the same underneath.' I noticed that she was always dressed whenever my friends' fathers came to pick them up. Simon's father, Frank Stiles, would drive up a few minutes earlier than he should have done to try and catch her out. When he arrived, he would scrutinise her with a frustrated squint of the eyes, as if he'd been anticipating a visit to a shop that had inexplicably closed down since his last call.

Whilst Mother was busy, The Great Caruso would be singing arias from a wood-panelled hi-fi system in the lounge. She only played one record, and didn't understand *that*, despite possessing a 'Learn Italian' LP. Annoyingly The Great Caruso never obliged, and persistently avoided all references to supermarkets and bus stations.

Indiscriminately she described each swelling aria as 'superb' without quite knowing why. She hated my father's extensive and beloved collection of jazz 78s, and fell asleep in films, even during *The Cruel Sea*, and the first film she ever took me to at the cinema, *Thunderball*.

'When your father and I used to live in Stratford,' Mother informed me, 'we went to the cinema free of charge.'

I was only six years old, and the sheer luxury of the privilege opened my mouth wide in admiring reverence. 'How?' I croaked.

'I used to work for J. Arthur Rank.'

I never knew she was friendly with the muscly man who hit the gong. 'And *he* let you in free?'

Mother ignored the question. 'We had a cat which I used to drape around my shoulders and pretend it was a fur. It always came with us, asleep on my neck.'

My mother acquired god-like status, and for many years I imagined her walking through the doors of any cinema in the country, dripping with a fur that only she and my father knew was really a napping cat. It came as something of a disappointment when we all had to pay the same as everyone else to see *Thunderball*. When I went to get the Maltesers I wanted to say who I belonged to, believing the cinema management would be embarrassed that they hadn't recognised my mother, and shamed into handing over the chocolates with apologetic haste.

Neither could I understand why the seats we had were situated at the side of the balcony, with a partially restricted view.

My mother talked throughout the film, and was more concerned with clearing up everybody else's sweet wrappers than watching the screen. When she had gathered a substantial handful of litter, she would screw it up into a tight ball with an exaggerated crinkling noise and make her way back along the row before depositing the papers into a rubbish bin. This would happen several times during the course of the afternoon, and Mother would quickly and savagely silence anybody who dared to mutter as she shuffled past them yet again; 'Well you shouldn't have bloody dropped it in the first place.'

We usually walked home from the cinema. Mother told me that she couldn't see the point of *Thunderball* but that you could 'tell someone by the amount of rubbish around them'.

Our walk took us through the town centre, which had been stolen from a crumbling, labyrinthine network of eighteenth-century shops. The new open plan was all plate glass and conveniently situated shrubs. Local hostility to the project had been numbed by a visit from the Queen, who had opened the Civic Centre. We had all bought Union Jack flags and run down to the end of our road where the Conservative Club stood. As the Queen passed in a large black car, we waved at her and were sure that she had noticed us. Especially us. Mother told me not to be so 'bloody silly'. A whole morning of expectation was over in about five seconds. The flag in my hand felt foolish, and I let it drop to the ground.

Across the main road from this complex was The Red Lion pub and Tustin the Master Butcher's. My mother didn't believe in spending money on good meat, but my grandparents would go there to buy chicken and kidneys every Saturday. To the right of the pub was the boys' school. The front entrance was further along the road, but from this angle you could see a full-sized model of a modern fighter plane guarding the back gate. The local papers were swollen by news of a drugs scandal there, and Mother didn't know what the place was coming to, although she still allowed its Scout Troop to sweep her leaves during Bob-a-Job week.

Between the pub and the school was a path which slithered alongside the hospital and the nurses' home. Hot, steaming pipes ran parallel with the path, and barbed wire coiled aorund them. The boy next door but seven had taken a short cut through the hospital a few weeks ago, and had fallen on to the pipes, cutting and scorching his thigh. I didn't believe that doctors could sew people back up with a normal needle and thread, so I gave him my Sherbet Fountain to make him feel better. As the pipes hissed and popped, I wondered what Mother might have given me if I'd thrown myself on to them.

At the end of the path, we turned right. The council were building a new pregnancy centre. I thought this was where girls went to get babies, but Mother said that they only went there to make sure everything was all right once they had already got them.

'So where do the babies come from?'

Mother considered. 'From ladies' tummies,' she replied. It was not something I wished to pursue.

We crossed the road opposite the pregnancy centre and went to visit Aunty Betty and Uncle Jack.

We always visited Aunty Betty, though Mother thought that Uncle Jack was 'harsh and rather sour'. I was given a banana milkshake when I went there, which was the kind of wild pleasure denied at our house. A large, friendly mongrel called Penny greeted us. She was forever moulting. A trip to Aunty Betty's was never complete without Mother making use of the small nozzle on the Hoover when we returned home.

Aunty Betty had usually had a spiritual experience between my mother's last visit and the current one. She was convinced that Jesus was alive and in her back garden, preparing for what she described as His 'Second Comeback'. My mother listened to the latest details with rapt attention, brown eyes moist with emotion.

'There there, my dear,' she said, holding Betty's hand tightly but tenderly in her own densely jewelled fingers.

'I think He's somewhere near the shed,' Aunty Betty continued. 'Certainly not as far back as the compost heap, but more so than the bit where Penny goes to the toilet.'

'There, there . . .'

'I'll just play you my latest recording,' she went on, fixing Mother with a beatific smile and a stare from two blue china-plate eyes. Her cheeks glowed a bright cherry red as she fumbled with the tape recorder, eventually deciding that she was ready to begin. Normally, Aunty Betty would play back readings of selected passages from the Bible, and my mother would stare thoughtfully into the middle distance and say, 'Lovely. Really superb.' But this time, the recital was a poem by John Donne, which included the lines,

> 'For oughtest thou, O Lord, despise us thus,
> And to be utterly enrag'd at us?'

'Very true, Betty. Very true,' my mother managed after a short and poignant pause. She shook slightly with emotion.

Aunty Betty also had dreams, or 'visions of rest' as she preferred, and produced small oil paintings that were 'inspired' by them. The walls of her bedroom were peppered with orange landscapes cut through with purple rivers and lime-green pathways. My mother was fulsome in her praise, especially consider-ing (as she always pointed out) that Betty had never received any proper training.

Mother was an entirely pragmatic woman who couldn't contend with such an intensely spiritual dimension to life, although she tried hard enough to keep up with Aunty Betty's unflagging fervour. A print of Dürer's *Praying Hands* hung above her side of the bed, and she often pronounced it as 'smashing'. She even managed dreams of her own, although they always seemed to involve the intricate mapping of foreign capitals. Remarkable as these might have been, on no account could the carefully recounted street names of central Istanbul be described as a 'vision' of the same magnitude as Aunty Betty's visitations.

I'd noticed that many of my mother's friends seemed to be ill or immobilised in some way. My world was awash with broken bodies and decaying tissue. Aunty Betty herself had funny legs, and was confined to bed for much of the day, although I can still remember her being able to drive her black Ford Poplar to the shops. I habitually tried to sneak a look, believing them to have the appearance and texture of jelly.

Aunty Pam Wilson was always having operations and, from what I'd been told, there wasn't much more of her to cut out.

Mrs Frings, who only lived a few houses up the road, had problems 'inside her head'. Mother was less willing to give her sympathy to Mrs Frings because there wasn't really anything to see. I was told to smile whenever she said something I didn't understand. One day, while sitting in our back garden, she turned to my mother and said, 'I can talk normally now.'

My mother sipped her sherry, and replied sweetly, 'Well of course you can.'

'No. It's easier outside. They can't hear me.'

'Can't they? That's good.'

'The doctors. They've got your house bugged. But not out here in the garden. They didn't think I'd come out here, you know.'

'I bet they didn't.' Mother shot me a warning glance, and I remembered to smile.

We tended not to worship on Sundays, though every now and then there was a minor flirtation with the Baptist Church in Acock's Green. We would take two cars, so that my father could go straight on to the office afterwards.

Next door was a police station where they still stabled horses. Sometimes our arrival would coincide with the horses returning from their morning exercise. There were about twenty of them, bright and steaming in the fragile morning air. They would always leave a mess in front of the church's wooden doors, and my mother would always make a joke to the vicar about something called 'the offering'. He would smile and say that God was pleased to receive anything, so long as it was offered in the right spirit.

Because we went so infrequently, I didn't like 'the divide', when all 'the little ones' disappeared into another room behind the pulpit whilst something mysterious happened with the adults out front. I assumed that God in person had been waiting in the wings, and that only grown-ups were allowed to see Him. The instruction for us to go backstage was a signal for Him to confront the congregation. It was another example of children being denied access to the unfathomable workings of adult life, and I wondered how God got in. I imagined he was hiding in the church's wooden ceiling rafters, and would lower Himself down at the appropriate moment. Mother would only tell me that God was there, in a manner of speaking, and that everybody had a biscuit and a drink with Him.

The little ones were working their way systematically through the Bible stories. The gaps in my knowledge meant that the usual narrative logic and the connections between the Old and New Testaments were lost to me. A masculine woman with a large nose took the classes and, like an anti-aircraft gun, her attention swivelled to me whenever I attended.

'Now, children.' She looked directly at me. 'As certain of our number has made one of his rare appearances, would someone like to tell him what we did last week?'

A small boy with glasses put his hand up.

'Ronald?'

'The blinding of Samson, Miss.'

I perked up.

'Very good, Ronald. Now, before Samson was made blind, he had his hair cut off. Can you think why that might have been?'

There was no doubt who was expected to answer.

The other children waited expectantly.

'Because it was too long?'

Miss trembled slightly. 'But *why* was it too long? That's the question.'

This was tricky. I did my best. 'Because he didn't cut it very often.' Miss was clearly dissatisfied, so I added, 'Maybe he was on drugs. The Rolling Stones have long hair, and they're on drugs. They smoke, too. But the Beatles are OK. My dad's got some of their records.'

My early religious education was, at best, patchy. It encompassed the Creation, then moved swiftly through to Noah, Moses and King David. A few details supplemented these oases of enlightenment, but beyond bushes that were burnt or seas that were parted, there was a blank until the Nativity, and then nothing again until the Crucifixion. I knew about Jesus walking on water and about some miracles. I even did a small project on the overturning of the money-lenders' tables, but I never knew enough to sense the overall pattern behind each individual event.

Miss told me that Saint Stephen was stoned to death. 'And that's what will happen to you. Stoned in the pebbles of ignorance.'

My mother told me to take no notice, and that we only went to that church because 'your father's bloody parents say they're Baptists – although, of course, you never see *them* there'.

'And anyway,' she continued, 'that's the way it is. It's like life. Manage it as best you can, but there aren't really many things worth remembering. Not really. Not when you come down to it.'

Although Mother tried to keep abreast of Aunty Betty's religious zeal, Sundays weren't really for church in our family. She couldn't be doing with intrusions on her life, and my father was probably pleased to be excused for part of the day.

Quite often, though, my parents used to have early cocktail parties. Neither of them liked parties, but it somehow seemed important to do something communal on a Sunday morning.

My mother was an expert with potato salad. On these occasions, she produced basinfuls of it, and filled

15

the kitchen with neat piles of carefully mangled potato, mayonnaise, pickled gherkin and onion. She would also allow both downstairs rooms to be used at the same time; for the rest of the year – excluding Christmas Day – one of them would be kept in dark cold storage. To maintain discipline in this matter, my mother would remove the fuse that controlled the heat and light in whichever room was dormant. Once, she miscalculated and disconnected the power to the tropical fish tank, killing over twenty fish. 'Never mind,' she said, 'the cat can have them,' and scooped them all into a copy of the *Sunday Express*.

The same people would always turn up to these functions, but they would never bring their children. I was released into a forest of trousers legs, zips and swaying handbags, and told to 'get rid of the potato salad, at all costs . . .' When it was really hectic, I was allowed a go with the soda-siphon. 'But don't drown the drinks,' mother instructed, 'except for Uncle Lance's. Put an extra squirt in for him, just in case.'

Uncle Lance Cohen was a very short man. The only person in the room shorter than him was his wife, Aunty Kath. She sat at the far end of the room, her squashy features and compressed posture giving her the look of a frog. Her dress was too short, and rode up over her bony thighs, exposing the darker portion of the tan-coloured tights she was wearing. She was talking to Aunty Betty, who was in the next chair, two walking sticks propped up behind it.

'We once had someone come into the café,' Aunty Kath was saying, 'who claimed he was Jesus. I reckon he was only after a free egg and chips, though.'

Aunty Betty smiled generously. 'But he could have been. Jesus is everywhere, after all. Most of the time He's in our back garden, but he could be in your café, too.'

'But why would Jesus choose the Top Cat Café in Knowle? Surely He'd go to Jerusalem, or somewhere like that.'

Uncle Lance was also talking about the man who'd said he was Jesus. 'Steady with that soda, son. Now, where do you think Jesus would come back to?'

I thought for a minute. 'The tax office,' I replied. 'He could work there so that Dad's business wouldn't have to pay any tax.'

Uncle Peter Peters looked dismayed at the mention of tax. He had hairy eyebrows that curled up and round in front of a sharp, acquisitive face. He was one of my father's friends from the jewellery business. He took another handful of nuts and asked me what I knew about tax. 'Not very much,' I replied, shyly. 'But I know that Dad always goes away when the tax man comes to look at his books.' I was encouraged by the laughter that came from the small group of grown-up people who were now surrounding me. 'And Mum goes to the office with perfume and a dress that shows off her bosoms. She says she'll be the one that deals with him because Dad's bloody hopeless at that sort of thing.'

My father was talking with Uncle George Banks, who came round to our house every Tuesday morning to pick up something called 'the stock'. He always bought me a Bounty, and had recently caught on to the fact that I liked the ones with a dark chocolate coating. I took my father a bottle of Coca-Cola. He never drank alcohol as it did something funny to his stomach. Occasionally, he would have a rum and Coke, though this was only because he could fill his glass with Coke without having to really taste the spirit.

They were talking about Uncle Dennis Moore. My father had told me that we wouldn't be seeing him again because he'd had to send him off to another job. Uncle Dennis had left seven thousand pounds' worth of diamond rings in the boot of his Humber Snipe, and somebody had stolen the lot.

Mr Frings was talking to my mother. She was smoking, and drinking what she called 'Lambrusci'. Mr Frings had an enormous plate of potato salad in one hand, and a bowl of home-made trifle in the other. He was a sad-looking man who reminded me of a cocker-spaniel. They were talking in German. Mother was a different person whenever she spoke her native language. She smiled and relaxed with people, nodding her head as she sucked in the words of agreement; 'JA, JA . . .' she was saying, although each syllable was pronounced with a whispered hush and took what seemed like several seconds to pronounce. 'Yes, yes . . .' she said, but it still sounded like a death rattle.

I went into the kitchen and started to play with the four plastic models of The Beatles that my father had brought back from Liverpool the week before. Uncle Lance came in. 'Ah, young man. You don't know where your mother keeps the drink do you?'

I told him that I'd seen some spare bottles in the outside toilet last week. He nodded.

'Which one is your favourite?' he asked, gesturing at the Fab Four.

'I like Ringo. Even though his arm has come off. He's the funny one.'

'What about the others?'

'John's too serious. Paul's very boring. I like George, though. He seems nice.'

'Would you like to be a pop star?'

I said that it would be all right, except for all the girls chasing after me.

'But I bet you'd like to earn a lot of money?'

I sensed a trap, but thought honesty was the best policy: 'Yes,' I eventually agreed.

Uncle Lance didn't give up easily. 'And what would you spend it on?'

'I'd buy Dad some new stock. I think Uncle Dennis lost some of it. And Mum needs a new bra.'

'And for yourelf?'

'An E-type Jag.'

'Have you put on weight?' Uncle Lance asked.

'Have you shrunk?'

'I don't think you've got The Beatles in the right order.' He ignored the last comment. 'John should be on the left as we look at them. Do you know which is your left? And Paul should be in the middle . . . let me . . .'

I left him, picked up another large basin's worth of potato salad and wandered back through the hall. I met Mother coming the other way, looking anxious and clutching the soda-siphon tightly to her.

'Have you seen Uncle Lance?' she asked.

'He's in the kitchen, playing with The Beatles.'

'Don't be bloody daft,' but she went into the kitchen anyway.

After everybody had left, Mother stripped down to her underwear to start the clearing-up operations. It was Sunday, after all.

The empty Chianti bottles that were strung up around the lounge were taken down, and the cheese plant moved back to the hall. The glass doors dividing the 'usable' room from the 'dormant' one were once more slid into place, and polish wiped vigorously over them.

'Frank's a bit of a fatty these days,' Mother said. 'I was worried when he started to lean on these doors. I thought he was going straight through.'

With mechanical precision she removed all the fuses from the room we weren't going to use, tapped the barometer on her way out, and bolted the door.

The kitchen was full of piled plates and dirty glasses. I was allowed to dry them when there had been a big turn-out. My father was in the lounge, reading the football reports in *The Sunday Times*.

I asked mother what she had been saying to Mr Frings.

'He was telling me about his time in the Navy during the war. He drove torpedoes at enemy ships.'

'You mean English ships – our ships?' I said.

'Whatever. Enemy ships.'

'But why wasn't he killed?'

'He used to jump off at the last minute. I think it's had a funny effect on him.'

'Is that why he's come to England?'

Mother peeled off her yellow rubber gloves and blew energetically into them. When inflated, they looked like toads with antlers.

'Why don't you teach me to speak German?' I asked with great deliberation. 'Then I could talk to Mr Frings too.'

It was a question I'd asked several times already during my short life. My mother had a kind of superficial enthusiasm for the whole thing, but would never actually take time to teach me properly. She insisted on speaking German quickly in intense, concentrated bursts, perhaps knowing that I would lose interest either through self-consciousness or an inevitable sense of ignorant humiliation. Instead, I grew to know the language without her help, scavenging it from television, comics and overheard coffee-time gossip during our frequent holidays to Germany.

She picked up her mug of sherry, and I tried to outflank her.

'Mum, what does "Hummel Hummel" mean?'

She explained that it was an insult shouted at the old watercarriers in Hamburg, where she was brought up. After a while, they got fed up with being taunted, so they devised a response.

'What was that?' I asked.

'They said, "Mors Mors."' She paused. 'I suppose it means "Arse Arse".'

'You mean like Dad's?' I said.

'Something like Dad's,' she replied and, for a moment, looked almost wistful.

Dear Rainer,

You see, I keep my word. There will always be some time left over for you. And I miss our talks. Nonetheless, I have seen more cheerfulness over this past week or so than I ever did in the three years we spent together. I would be the first to say that this was not your fault – the war made things difficult. There is rationing in England, but not as severe as in Germany. I shall send food or some clothes, when I can get hold of them.

The family is kind enough, although the Frau is stand-offish. She doesn't trust me yet. Last week, she planted her gold charm bracelet in a tin of tea. When I 'found' it for her, she claimed that she'd put it there ages ago and must have forgotten, but I saw her wearing it only the other day and knew immediately she was telling whoppers.

The children, Nicholas and Raymond, are spoilt devils. They don't like my cooking, but that's their lookout. In the morning I do the housework; wiping, washing, dusting, putting out, putting away, shining and straightening – the lot. Drudgery, but Mama's thumpings with that poker trained me to be thorough – I can do it all easy as pissing. I think the Reverend and Mrs Bacon are pleased with my little efforts. So they should be.

I have started to read again, and have even tried sketching the view from my bedroom window. Green fields and hills, a small winding road, puffy trees, bicycles, people. Nothing really. I'd forgotten you could hear the quiet.

There is a river which I can swim in, but compared to the Elbe, it's nothing more than a grey piddle. Do you remember splashing across to the other half of our village on the opposite bank? No doubt it's still deserted – I can't see the bloody Russians ever shifting. In the cold weather your balls looked like acorns. A car has just come into the drive; at least we have petrol! No doubt I will be expected to smile a lot. The Bacons like their tame German to show 'fortitude in adversity'. At the moment, I am not even dressed.

Goodbye, Rainer: I love you – as much as I ever did.

Nr. Stratford. August 4th, 1947.

– 2 –

My mother was on the telephone to my father. She was gulping back small but persistent mouthfuls of sweet sherry while she talked, and the radio was getting a good going over with the yellow duster, which was liberally smeared with an opaque creamy substance.

My father was, as usual, at the office, safely away on the other side of Birmingham. 'I'm going to the Post Office with the registereds, then I've a bit more work to do.'

'So you'll be late?' Even then, I knew that there shouldn't have been a question mark there.

'Yes.'

'How are you getting to the Post Office?'

My father sighed. It wasn't enough that my mother should determine exactly what clothes he wore every day, or that his eating habits were entirely dictated by the ominous bundles of white springy bread, margarine strata and over-fatty Continental meats that were deposited in his briefcase at a quarter to eight every morning. Even at the office, he was not wholly outside her sphere of influence.

'I'll drive,' he replied, with what sounded like mild impatience.

'In the car?' my mother pressed.

'Of course. Yes. In the car.'

'You could walk. It would do you good. You're getting a bit paunchy.'

'I could. But it's starting to rain.'

'And you don't want to get wet?'

There was a pause while my father calculated what kind of question this was. At length he tried, 'No.'

'Oh well. Suit yourself. But it would do you good. What about your tea?'

A rare and welcome break from German liver sausage beckoned to my father. 'I'll get something here,' he said, as innocuously as possible.

'At the fish and chip shop . . .'

'Yes . . .'

'. . . just up the road?'

The construction had a misleading tenderness about it. 'Yes,' my father replied, as directly as he dared. And then with renewed confidence, 'I'll just stroll up there after I've come back from the post.'

Mother was triumphant. 'What? In this weather?'

These telephone calls, at about four o'clock every day, were my mother's way of reminding father about his place in the hierachy. She was a great one for hierarchies; everything had its place and had to be kept in order. We always knew, for example, that the cleaning fluids were to be found in the grill above the oven – nobody was allowed to use the grill, because it made a mess. The cans of cola were hidden in the outside toilet, and were never moved, years after I'd first discovered them. Every year, Christmas presents accumulated on top of my father's wardrobe. But his prolonged stays at The Office threatened the neatness of my mother's system as he was somehow anarchically out of reach, despite her attempts to regulate his existence from home.

The Office had acquired a mysterious attraction for me long before I can remember my first actual visit there. The drive across town and through the meandering back streets of Handsworth only made the voyage that much more interesting and secretive. Unaccountably, my father had several different routes, and would sometimes stop in the middle of out-of-the-way housing estates, to 'just nip out for a few moments', or, more plausibly, to 'buy a paper'.

The building itself was set in a row of piled Victorian villas, except that my father's factory extended far out at the back, and reminded me of a ship. My grandfather had moved the family business away from the jewellery quarter thirty years ago, 'before the Blacks really got a grip' my mother would remind me and anybody else who cared to listen.

Inside, it resembled what I could remember of Fagin's hideout in *Oliver*. It sprawled across a number of levels and irregularly-shaped rooms, which somehow didn't create a coherent whole. The bottom floor spread across four workshops. This was where the dirty work was done, and there was always an impenetrable smell of sweat and ammonia. Aunty Beryl and Aunty Ruby were the polishers, and steadily worked their ways through ordered piles of diamond rings, wrapping and protecting the finished articles with small clouds of cotton wool. Brian did something called 'waxing', and was always wiping his hands down a brown, grease-smeared overall. I could never bring myself to call him Uncle Brian, as the real uncles all worked upstairs.

Uncle Peter and Uncle Lance wore white overalls, and Uncle Dennis and Uncle George wore suits.

One day, as I had finished exploring and Aunty Ruby had run out of sweets, I went to see my father in the front office. Just as I was about to go through the door, Unlce Lance caught me by the arm.

'Don't go in there just yet,' he hissed.

'Why not?' I said. 'I need my colouring things.'

'He's talking to Uncle Dennis. It's not something you want to hear,' he went on confidentially. 'Come and see how the rings are made, and get your colouring things later.'

Whilst Uncle Lance was steering me along the workshop benches, which were manned by a dozen or so men all called Bernard or Albert or Tom, I gazed at the calendars with pictures of naked women, who had been photographed on holiday at the seaside or whilst cleaning their cars. 'What are these?' I asked.

'They help the men to concentrate,' Uncle Lance replied.

'Like chewing-gum?' I offered.

'Sort of.'

All the men were busy blowing jets of flame through thin nozzles at gold rings which they held firmly but delicately with thick metal tweezers.

'Why are they doing that?'

Uncle Lance explained that the men were softening the metal so that they could make it the right shape

27

and size to go on people's fingers. I remembered my mother telling me of Old Albert who had sucked in at the wrong time and done his tubes no end of harm. Then I asked Uncle Lance if I could have some paper to draw on. He fetched some smart-looking A4 with my father's name embossed in brown ink at the top left hand corner, and I found an empty bench and drew a picture of Old Albert exploding in three separate stages. The last frame showed a vivid flash at the centre of the page, with Old Albert's limbs splayed over the rest of it. I finished the piece off by writing 'The End' underneath the amputated left leg.

When Uncle Dennis trooped out of my father's office he looked tired and rather angry. I ran up to him and offered my drawing. Uncle Dennis was a tall, thin man with a slim moustache and neatly creamed hair, the sort who acted the part of the British officer in war films. Stoically, and without too much of a grimace, he passed his eye over Old Albert exploding.

'It's upside down,' I said, after a rather awkward silence.

Uncle Dennis became thoughtful. 'Does it really matter?' he smiled, and stared at the fire extinguisher which had never worked on the opposite wall.

I wondered whether he meant for Old Albert or the sake of the drawing itself, but never got the chance to find out. Uncle Dennis walked stiffly past me, looking as if he was about to cry. I never saw him again, but many years later I heard my father say that he'd opened an ironmonger's shop in Bournemouth.

★

When I got home, my mother was just slipping her apron on after an upstairs Hoover. Aunty Betty was also there, smiling seraphically between heavily lipsticked lips and fingering a cassette with the words 'Colloquies with Christ: The Bedroom' clearly printed on its label.

I asked Aunty Betty whether men could cry, and she said that of course they could, if their spirits were greatly affected. My mother broke in, 'It's only Dennis. He wanted his job back. He should have thought about that before he left his bloody boot open.'

Aunty Betty was clearly distressed, and whispered something about forgiveness. There was no stopping my mother, though.

'We all have to face the consequences of our actions. Dennis did wrong. He was probably drunk at the time, anyway. You can tell when he's had too many – eyes like piss-holes in the snow.'

Aunty Betty looked inside her handbag for a Biro, which she then brought out, but for no apparent purpose. 'All the same, my dear,' she eventually said, 'I'm sure he didn't mean to.'

Mother poured herself a sherry. Aunty Betty had touched on unfamiliar metaphysical territory, so she asked about her latest encounter with the Almighty, who had apparently ventured indoors due to the unsettled weather.

I received your letter and am, of course, relieved that you are so well, even though the post seems to take a frustratingly

*devious route. Space and Time separate us. I have suspicions
that letters and parcels are still being 'investigated' by the
English and Americans, and wonder if the Americans' sense
of propriety is as well developed as it should be. For their
part, however, the English seem mildly embarrassed by the
desolation and the evidence of violence which persists here
(despite their efforts to tidy it all away), two years since that
treaty was signed. Only a few miles up the road. Such hope
then.*

*The Americans remember you and occasionally bring your
parents food and clothing. Since you left, however, their
ardour has cooled for these particular acts of benevolence.
Your Captain Fitzgerald – still reminding us all of his Irish
ancestors – arrived the other day whilst I was helping your
father mix some cement. He didn't lend a hand, but did ask
how long you were going to be away. 'As long as it takes,'
I said.*

*'She oughta come to the States. She'll make money
quicker. What's she doing anyway? Looking after some
priest's kids. There's not much in that.' Certainly his
freckles had been brought out by the exchange.*

*I know he still feels pity for us. It is not an emotion he's
comfortable with. I'm not sure we will see him (much)
again.*

*With your mother's robust help, your father is getting
stronger by the day. His distrust of the Americans remains
deep and stubborn. He is pleased that you are in England.*

*He told me something which helps to explain his feelings.
As you know, he is full of his stories, but it is the first time
I've heard this one. Do not be alarmed or angry; I regard
the following revelation as evidence that he is coming to
terms with his experiences. Its 'release' seems to have*

coincided with an end to those nightmares, just as our old friends Freud and Jung had it. Your mother, at least, is relieved. Any more of his thrashing about, and I'm certain he would have been banned to the kitchen flagstones.

Your father actually escaped from the Russian prison camp in 1944. By some miracle, or perhaps a series of them (he jokes that he's used up all his miracles in one go, like a cat's nine lives) he managed to crawl to the American lines. It took him almost a week; he couldn't stand up because of the posture of his body in the cramped cell.

He gave himself up to the first GI encountered. The highest ranking officer was a lieutenant, and eventually your father found him, after passing through the hands of a compassionate sergeant (who gave him a cigarette) and a well-meaning corporal. The corporal offered him some chewing-gum – he obviously couldn't see inside your father's mouth, where the Russians had performed their brutal dentistry with a rifle butt.

At first, the lieutenant also seemed helpful. He ordered that your father be cleaned up, given new clothes and fed, as well as the state of his mouth and stomach permitted. Whilst these acts of generosity were being administered, the officer was engaged in earnest conversation on a field telephone with someone who was evidently a superior officer. Eventually, he came over to your father again, shamefaced and apologetic, and said that they would have to send him back to the Russians(!)

I suspect your father broke at this point. 'Do you know what they will do to me?' he demanded, and he pleaded for a change of heart. The lieutenant could only say that it was important for American relations with Russia that he shouldn't poach their prisoners, especially those they seemed especially interested in. There were, apparently, already signs of strain in their liaison, and isolated incidents such as this could be exaggerated at a later date and used to undermine American influence and intention.

The long and short of it is that your father was returned to the Russian camp, and punished for his troubles. I do not intend to shake the details from him – I daresay they will emerge in time, and then 'suddenly', like a cork jettisoned from a bottle after careful, sensitve manipulation. As I write, he is happily at work with a spirit level. Your house is coming on well. Everybody in the village is busy rebuilding their homes, although there aren't really enough materials, and people are having to reuse old bricks, picking their way through the piles of rubble to find the whole ones and then chipping away old cement. There is talk of a brick factory opening further down the Elbe, and your father is confident of getting a job there. For obvious reasons, there are going to be a reasonable number of jobs for only a relative handful of men.

How fortunate we are to be on this side of the river. The other half of the village you can recall swimming over to is no longer that landscape of barns, shops and houses. Watch-towers and fences have appeared in the last two weeks, and I'm certain that even the smaller beaches have been mined. Even the Allies are getting edgy, and regularly patrol the Elbe road. They say that they will stay here so long as the Russians seem to be a threat. Your father thinks the Americans will pull out whenever it is most convenient to them. 'They do not care about the German people,' he says, 'or any people. They only worry about themselves.'

All this must seem rather forbidding, but it's not all bad. When you return, you will see significant changes.

Your first letter seemed optimistic, though I would relish more. You say little of the people you are staying with – 'that priest' as Captain Fitzgerald calls him – apart from the wife's reserve. I am learning to be patient and not ask too many questions, but I would appreciate anything you could say about life in England, particularly of Wittgenstein. Is he still in Cambridge? English people might find it hard to understand a German being interested in an Austrian Jew, but there we are.

In return, I send your parents' love . . . and a heartfelt embrace from your beloved Rainer.

Luneburg. August 29th, 1947.

The kitchen clock had been set fifteen minutes fast so that we all had more time to do things. That evening, on the stroke of what would have been five o'clock, as was the habit on Saturday, I had beans on toast for tea. It wasn't quite like other peoples' beans on toast, because my mother always prepared meals well ahead to save time and to make her feel 'organised'. The beans had been in the saucepan since mid-morning, and were simply reheated. The toast had been done at the same time, which meant it was hard and brittle. My mother compensated for this by layering margarine on to it with extravagant sweeps of the butter knife. More often than not, bread and margarine were substituted for the toast, as the toaster was really an ornament and the grill was packed with Brillo pads, a medium-sized bottle of Brasso and other cleaning fluids.

'What will Uncle Dennis do now that Dad's not giving him any money?' I asked.

'He'll find something. Probably be better off in the long run. They all are.'

'Did Aunty Betty think God would be angry with us?'

Mother considered. 'I don't think God's interested in Dennis or what he lost from the back of the Humber. I shouldn't worry if I were you. Worse things have happened at sea.'

'Did you ever have any other jobs, Mum?'

She seemed overwhelmed with memories for a while before saying, 'I used to do some translating for the Americans at the end of the war.'

I remembered my English grandfather. 'Is that the war where Tatters got his left nipple shot off?'

'No. The next one. The second one,' she said firmly. 'And I used to be a stripper.'

This really was a revelation. I tried to contain my admiring excitement. 'You mean you used to take your clothes off in front of people?'

'Of course. I danced with two sets of feathers – one for the back and one for the front, with no clothes underneath. The trick was to flap them around so that nobody could quite see what they were looking for.'

I tried to picture the scene, with my mother slipping gingerly out of her blue chequered apron and brown cardigan and immediately concealing her body with two large sets of pink feathers. Before my imagination got the better of me, she said, 'Eat your beans, and don't tell Aunty Betty.'

*

As far as The Office went, that year was a difficult one. As well as Uncle Dennis going, Uncle George left a case of rings in Streatham and the supply of Bounties dried up. My father used to arrive home with bad headaches, and there was talk of having to sell the house. I offered to make some perfume from the roses in the back garden and sell that to help raise money, and I wondered if *Blue Peter* might hold an appeal. Aunty Betty gave me a shilling for one of the bottles – a prototype containing crushed brownish rose petals and smelling like my father's rum hair pomade – and Aunty Sylvia who lived next door said she'd buy one when the mix was ready. My mother smiled kindly when I handed the money over, but I sensed that it wasn't really doing much good.

The main effect of all this was that my grandfather retired at the age of seventy-five. He was reluctant, but everybody else was rather delighted, or relieved, or both. My father said that he'd been the cause of his headaches, and called him a liability. 'It's a cut-throat business now,' he told me, 'and Tatters is too old for it.'

I felt sorry for the old man. We all called him Tatters because when he went for a walk, he would ask if anyone wanted a 'tatters'. He was a short man with plenty of gold teeth who always dressed smartly. He often used a walking stick and wore a hat, which he used to raise to people he knew, and as the years caught up with him, many that he didn't. Tatters was married to Nanna, who was thin and severe-looking. My mother often told me that Nanna was selfish and cruel and a 'tough old bird', though she was kind to me.

'She's milked that business dry, and now look where we are,' she said. 'How many times a year do they go to bloody Torquay? That's what I'd like to know.'

'It's not really a question of Torquay,' my father replied evenly, and with heavily camouflaged defiance.

'And have you seen her furs? And those spindly fingers – covered in great ruddy diamonds. And we have to make do whilst Her Ladyship lives the life of Riley.'

I wasn't sure who Riley was, but I thought he must be quite rich. However, I did know that my mother had some furs as well, though admittedly they were not in Nanna's class. She had a fox fur and two minks, none of which she ever wore. They lay in her wardrobe smelling of the mothballs I'd swallowed when only a baby. Their mouths were wide open, neutral glass eyes staring out of the gloom and occasionally catching the light. I understood why she never put them on.

Whenever I asked my mother why she disliked Nanna so much, she would narrow her eyes, and say coldly, 'She never took to me. She never welcomed me when I came over from Germany. She never helped when you were born. Only the best for Lady Muck, but any old rubbish would do for me.'

Still, I couldn't help liking her, although there seemed to be something in what my mother said. Nanna would not travel on public transport, and a man called Bill used to run her to the shops every

Tuesday and Thursday, one day for the 'essentials', and one for the more biblical stuff, like bread, meat and fish. Eggs were always bought from a farm in the country, which particularly annoyed my mother. 'Eggs are eggs,' she would say. 'What's wrong with the ones the rest of us eat?'

Tatters was no longer allowed to drive. He'd bought a driving license years before you had to pass a test, and now the insurance companies refused to deal with him. He'd once damaged nine cars at a car park in Caernarvon trying to reverse his Ford Zephyr into a small space. On another occasion, he had knocked over close to a dozen dustbins which were waiting to be emptied, all perched on the edge of the pavement and each firmly nudged as he drove the Zephyr too close to the kerb. When people shouted at him, Tatters politely raised his hat and smiled at each in turn.

Sometimes I was miserable. Tatters no longer played football with me, and Dr Powell-Tuck used to visit him every Sunday afternoon to look at the trouble-some nipple, and at another wound in his left ankle. My mother told me that he'd actually been very lucky.

'The bullet went right through. It only shattered the bone,' she said.

'Ah,' I replied, not certain whether or not I should have been disappointed.

She rolled up her sleeve and showed me a scar on her forearm about the same size and shape as a large orange segment. '*That's* shrapnel,' she said, 'and this happened at the same time.' In one fluent movement, she put her hand to her mouth and pulled out her two front teeth, which were attached to a transparent mould that held them in place. There were little slithers of gherkin on its underside. 'He was lucky,' she confirmed. 'My shrapnel almost cost me my looks.'

Whatever my mother's afflictions, I couldn't help feeling more sorry for Tatters. He seemed to be getting shorter, his nipple ached and my father was always bad-tempered when he tried to stop him coming to the office.

Despite this embargo, Tatters continued with his pen and ink sketches of ring and brooch patterns, exquisitely designed and delicately tinted with colours from an antique box of watercolour paints. He called me into his study, and showed me his sketch books. Each page was separated by a fine piece of tissue paper. Everything was precious and treated as such. For me, this was an unaccustomed feeling. I stopped at one of the pages and asked what the exotic design was.

'A scarab beetle.'

'Ah.'

'The Egyptians thought they were sacred.'

I had seen something on television the week before. 'Like the Seven Sacred Foreskins?'

'Very possibly,' he replied.

I asked why it had such a huge diamond in it. 'Beetles are never that size. Besides, Dad hasn't got anything that big.'

'That's the point,' Tatters said. 'He'll never be able to make it, not even if he wanted to.'

'Nanna's got diamonds as big as that. Mum says so,' I tried.

'Does she? I'm sure it's none of her business.'

We were just in time for lunch. I always went to lunch with Nanna and Tatters at the weekend. They enjoyed taking me from my mother's cooking and, even then, I was vaguely aware that I should be thankful.

'Why do you put your ice-cream on the boiler, Nanna?' I asked.

'To stop it getting too cold,' she said, 'and don't swallow those cherry stones. They'll grow inside your stomach, and then where will you be?'

I carefully picked out the small clusters of stones that I'd been teasingly hoarding in the sides of my mouth. 'Doesn't your mother teach you anything?'

My father had bought season tickets for us to watch the football. This made Tatters feel a bit better, though he still grumbled about not going to The Office.

He told me how he had gone to see Birmingham play in the Cup Final at Wembley in the 1930s. They had scored a goal, and Tatters had thrown his hat into the air like they did on the old newsreels. By the time it had come down again, the other side had also scored. 'But people don't wear hats today,' he said, 'they wear scarves. Even when it's hot, they still wear them.'

My father used to take us to the match in Tatters' car, as he wouldn't drive anything except a Mini. He picked us up after lunch, and Nanna said, 'You're always rushing. What did you have for lunch? It can't have been ready in time. I don't understand what goes on in that household. You ought to stay for a coffee and a ginger.'

Even though we sat in the posh seats, I felt a mixture of fear and excitement at this exposure to people who Nanna said 'wanted their heads examining'. The noise and the expectant, feverish mood outside the ground made me think of Aunty Betty's religious outings to Twickenham every year. She said that thousands of people were welcomed into the church at one go by a man from America with a loud voice and yellow teeth. 'Still, the Lord's only interested in the inside bits,' she would say, 'which is just as well for most of us.'

We had to park near the ground, because Tatters wasn't very good on his legs. Once there, he greeted anybody who glanced in his general direction, smiling and asking them how they were doing. I stayed close by, and started talking to my father or looking up at the floodlights.

Inside the ground, Tatters would sit down only to disappear to the toilet almost immediately, even if the game was about to start. Everybody who had just stood up and sat down for him a first time had to stand up again to let him past. Once past, he stood at the end of the row, and with gentlemanly deliberation headed off in the wrong direction, a bobbing head and regularly raised hat amongst thousands of indifferent, agitated fans. Often, he would disappear for half the match, resurfacing in the most unlikely places. Once, he had appeared in the press box behind me, to a chorus of, 'Come on, Grandpa – where are you meant to be?'

When a goal was scored, Tatters would stand up, look around, and say, 'Who scored? Was it Bridges?' – Bridges having transferred to Chelsea several years earlier.

My God, Rainer, you make unreasonable demands! No sooner do I arrive in England – barely settled in – and up you pop, wrinkling your nose as if you'd just left Papa's thunderbox, nagging for information. I've hardly had time to pee. And do I detect some jealousy? Don't worry; there are no Captain Fitzgeralds here – or any other Americans for that matter; they've all turned tail and gone home.

And you'll be glad to hear that life outside the house is restricted to what the Bacons allow, which is not much. It is all mundane, but safe. I suppose it gives me a sense of well-being. Mama was right – 'so long as you've got your health'; that's the most important thing. I'm satisfied just going to the shops (even for a scraggy piece of pork or a white, unappetising slab of butter) or walking down roads where buildings don't look like colanders, or being away from all those shit-coloured uniforms.

You see what has happened? You see what your wretched letter has done. Before I came to England, I had hopes of bundles of letters between us, criss-crossing Europe. I wondered whether that longing you keep on about might release

41

some feelings. Talk about corks! You have put me on the defensive with your nosing around. Do not fret, Rainer, simply because my romantic hopes have been dashed. You are no Abelard and (for God's sake!) I am certainly no Eloise. Remember this . . .

> *'You know the depths of shame to which my*
> *unbridled lust had consigned our bodies, with no*
> *reverence for decency or for God even during the*
> *days of Our Lord's Passion, or of the greater*
> *sacraments could keep me from wallowing in this*
> *mire.' (Fat chance!)*

The Reverend Bacon has a copy in his study – and between my improving English, and schoolgirl memories of the letters, I manage pretty well. You'd better be impressed.

I've decided to like Mrs Bacon, though I'm still not sure about him. (He laughs like a donkey.) She is considerate, and has collected most of the clothes and tins in the parcel with this letter. There are no more suspicions. I fished the bracelet out of the tea-tin right in front of her, and gave her what for. 'Mrs Bacon, I may be many things, but I am no thief,' I said. 'If I am going to live with you and look after your children then you will just have to trust me . . . Now, please put this somewhere more convenient.' Of course, I still keep my accent for little speeches like this.

Mrs Bacon didn't say a thing, but has taken it very well. I am a 'good German'. Although she is not an old person, her hands and toes are crippled and bent with arthritis. She finds it tiring to write, so I help with the parish administration. Mrs Bacon is a loyal supporter of her husband's vocation, but usually he takes her entirely for granted. Only last week, for example, I was playing with Nicholas and

42

Raymond in the garden. The Reverend Bacon was dozing in his deckchair; he sounded like a gurgling drain. A straw hat was folded down over his face (like that Aschenbach bugger), and he was listening to the cricket match being broadcast on the wireless from inside the house. Mrs Bacon, hardly ten metres away, was hard at work digging the vegetable patch! It was a hot day and – need I tell you? – she could barely grip the spade's handle. Rainer, I warn you now – never take me for granted like that, otherwise I'll be off.

The car that drew up contained Peter and Dulcie Slythe, friends of the Bacons. He is a small man, sharply dressed and with a thin, absolutely horizontal moustache smeared across his upper lip. A real runt, and smelling of cologne. Where does he get it? During the introductions, the Reverend reminded us all that the church couldn't do without 'dear old Peter's not inconsiderable support'. Apparently God even embraces scrap-metal. Then he clenched his teeth together in a kind of grimace that probably started out life as a smile many years ago, and laughed that long, braying note, 'Haaaaaaaa,' before adding his, 'dear, oh dear, dear.'

Dulcie is bigger than her husband (a lot bigger) – with dark-red hair piled high on a white face, slashings of scarlet lipstick and black mascara. Her eyes are large, wet and dark and seem to change colour depending on her mood. A bit of a tart, maybe, but her gliding walk gives the impression that she is some kind of ghost, or at least otherworldly. When I shook her hand, her palm felt warm and soft.

I served the tea, and was startled when I saw the whisky being poured out. As I was bending down to arrange things on the table, Dulcie Slythe suddenly took my hand again,

43

and before I could say anything, held the open palm towards the light. 'Surely she can't be soused already,' I remember thinking. She examined it carefully.

Oily Bacon soothed me. 'Dear, oh dear. It's all right. She's reading your fortune.'

'Intriguing,' Dulcie Slythe says.

'What do you see?'

'Many things.'

'Good things?' (Hopeful.)

A pause. 'Some good.'

Mrs Slythe took a set of well-thumbed cards from her handbag. She spread them out carefully on the table.

'Never make a decision without consulting her first,' Peter Slythe reassured me in his reedy litle voice.

'You are trapped between two worlds,' she said, 'and are not always sure which one you should choose.'

I listened politely.

'People consider you gregarious, even irresponsible – but I am not so sure. Men like you, and you tolerate their attentions.'

The Reverend Bacon was sippng his whisky, looking as if he was deep in thought. Probably pickled.

'You expect a great deal from life, dearie. More than it can provide, but less than you used to. You are . . . resigned, or becoming resigned.'

How can you be two things at once? Expectant and resigned? I'm sure I don't know.

'Thought and control' – that's what you say. Any behaviour that follows from these will eventually claim its own reward. I still believe in you. Don't even think about letting me down. All right, so the cards were interesting enough, but there we all were, in a priest's house, smoking

44

cigarettes, drinking whisky and listening to supernatural gossip! I don't think Reverend Bacon ought to be quite so familiar with Peter Slythe.

I said I'd see him at church on Sunday, and he replied, 'Oh, no. I'm not a church-going sort of chap.' Neither am I, but at least I go. It's best not to tempt Fate, and besides, you never know.

Write to me soon.

Nr. Stratford. September 11th, 1947.

The world began to open out. Aunty Betty called it my 'secular baptism', and Uncle Lance said it was the beginning of the end and that I had to mark his words. As well as the football, my father took me to the speedway, where I learnt to idolise riders like Nigel Boocock and Jim Lightfoot. Nigel Boocock wore blue feathers, which my mother thought 'showy', though she warmed to him when he lost three teeth in an accident.

But Uncle Lance was right. I began to feel uncomfortable. I didn't like the way people treated Tatters, but I thought it didn't really matter because so far I hadn't any cause to feel embarrassed about myself. I wondered whether it might happen, and eventually (of course) it did.

My mother said we had to go into the village.

'Do we have to?'

'Of course we do. You're old enough for long trousers now. Besides, you shouldn't be showing those warts.' I dared not look at the islands of compressed, dried, carbuncular skin on my knees.

I knew we were going to the shops because we walked past the Conservative Club rather than going the hospital way. Mrs Frings was crouching behind the hedge as we went past her house. When she heard what we were going for, she suggested that once the warts had cleared up (she said 'kleeert app'), lederhosen would be a good idea. Then she put a finger to her lips, looked anxiously about, and made a dash back to her front door.

'You've got to laugh,' my mother said, 'though lederhosen might be a good idea. Get Powell-Tuck to look at those warts next time he's round about your grandfather's nipple.'

We had a milkshake at Pattison's, and then went to Hitchcock's, the new department store. It was what Uncle Dennis would have called 'swanky', and my mother said, 'Smashing. Just like they have them in Germany.'

I asked if I could have new shoes as well.

'We've come for trousers. New shoes won't hide warts, you know.'

'But these hurt,' I tried.

'I won't let your father have more than one pair at a time. He manages all right. Why should you be different? You'll be wanting one of those flowery ties next.'

She found a pair of trousers in the sale. They had thin black and brown stripes down each leg, tapering

46

to a pair of stirrups just below the ankles. There was no zip or opening of any kind, and they clung to my waist and bottom in a revelatory, self-conscious manner.

'They're lovely,' my mother said. 'And smart. They're like riding trousers. Jockeys would wear those.'

'Girl jockeys,' I said. 'How am I going to go to the toilet?'

'The usual way. Just pull them down. No one will mind.'

'They're too tight.' I was desperate now.

'Wait a minute.' She went back to the hangers, and pulled off an identical pair. She thrust them at me whilst looking the other way. 'Try these.'

I put them on. The feminine curves disappeared, but they were now baggy round the thighs. I remembered an old film about golf I'd seen. 'I still can't go to the toilet.'

'You'll just have to be organised about it.'

She bought the trousers, and insisted that I wore them on the way home. We met someone from Aunty Betty's church in the food department. She was hovering by the spiced meats.

'Hello. My word – those are . . .' – the pause seemed to go on forever – . . .'elegant. Have you taken up riding?'

'No,' my mother said sharply. 'But we might go skiing. Come on, we've still got a lot to do.'

We walked out of the store. 'Why did you tell her we were going skiing – ?'

'Never you mind. But it shows how versatile your trousers are.'

We walked back past the hospital. I felt sure everybody was looking at me. At Aunty Betty's, whilst my mother was cleaning her handbag in the kitchen, I told her that I hated the trousers. Aunty Betty told me it didn't matter what I looked like on the outside.

'You always say that,' I said.

'That's because it's true.'

My mother came back into the room, and said she'd have to get another handbag as this one was filthy. At home, she had at least twenty-seven. I'd counted them whilst looking for presents last Christmas.

Aunty Betty said that I'd lost my innocence and was becoming vain. 'I'll say a prayer, though you've left Eden rather too early if you ask me.'

'And all over a pair of trousers,' my mother added. 'Why don't you see if you can manage the toilet?'

She put the trousers out for me every Saturday for the next year. I even got used to the whistles from the other children in the neighbourhood. Then my warts dropped off, and a pair of stiff lederhosen appeared. 'These'll last years,' my mother said with gusto. 'You can adjust them with these straps.' She pulled hard and hurt my shoulder.

For three years I was known as 'Plastic Pants' or 'Leather Nicks'. The leather shorts were indestructible.

Nanna thought it was a cruel shame and Aunty Betty saw it as a deserved hair shirt. My father smiled knowingly, grateful that he'd escaped into the comparative luxury of drip-dry shirts.

Your letter had given me heart. Despite Mrs Slythe and her magic cards, you seem to understand the people there. You must thank Mrs Bacon for the clothes that arrived with your letter; your mother, in particular, is pleased to have more than one dress again, and is quietly delighted that the colours in it are spectacularly unfaded. By nature she is not such an unremittingly floral sort of person, nonetheless, it has made her happy. The other women in the village – especially Frau Overath – are green. Nobody will say anything to her, but in unguarded moments we all perceive a flirtatious spring in your mother's purposeful stride.

With reference to Wittgenstein. I have heard from an educated British lieutenant that since he settled in Cambridge (in 1939), he has been revising his earlier comments in the Tractatus. *Take note – you may find what he says of some value. The rumour is this: we are told that language has a great variety of uses, like the tools in a carpenter's bag or a range of different games, each with its own equipment, rules, criteria of success and failure, and so on. The thesis goes that to understand anything, particularly any given use of language, we have to know what tool is being used, what game is being played. Any behaviour can only be judged in this respect; there are no all-embracing criteria of assessment to which we can appeal.*

My point is this: you are suspicious of what happens in the Reverend Bacon's house, yet you must also try to view behaviour from different perspectives. We inhabit different times and spaces than we used to; they are forever changing for us. Dare I ask you to contemplate the Cubists? Maybe not after last year's tantrums, but nevertheless as Germans ('good' or otherwise), we must learn to be more flexible. Just as Wittgenstein has come to see the inconsistencies of his

49

early beliefs, so we must also make allowances and, to use his analogy, learn new games.

So it is with the village, which is gradually coming back to life again, emerging from its long Stygian gloom. All of those who are going to return from camps have now done so; several families have lost hope, however, aware (no doubt) of the arbitrariness of Fate in such matters, but still prone to grief and persistent melancholy.

It strikes me as I consider their experiences, all (except Hinrichs) are showing signs of wear. Heinz has now become the blacksmith, though he has lost most of his hair and gained a pair of flapping jowls. Sadly, that renowned sense of humour has all but deserted him. Klink has become very fat (God knows how he's managed it), and in the absence of new clothes, is almost bursting out of his old ones. Herr Auschleck has taken to spectacles. Hinrichs alone remains physically unchanged, although he has developed an ingratiating, almost cringing manner that only emphasises the appearance of thrusting himself forward that he works so hard at avoiding. He has set up a general store, and is already driving hard bargains. Doubtless he will make a great success of the enterprise. Nobody wishes him well.

One of the consequences of the American presence is the new Black Market, where anything can be bought or bargained for (though I don't suppose we ought to complain too loudly – you did all right out of it before). I understand the need for 'healthy competition', but I fear we've been left too vulnerable, too soon, and can't fend for ourselves at this moment. Only the strongest will survive. What will happen to the others? Hinrichs, for example, has the only fruit for twenty kilometres; he knows about your father's teeth, and understands that until we get a dentist, he needs plums. He told me that he'd promised them to somebody else, but I know that he's exchanged them to buy a gift for Frau Holzenbein. There's no need to speculate about the terms of barter. In the end, I walked to Bleckede to get the stuff. It took almost a whole day.

Your family's house is slowly being built. You will recall the architectural difficulties of setting it on a slope – two storeys at the front, then three at the back, including a kitchen and cellars. It doesn't make things easy, but your father is quite boisterous. Late returners from the camps get no favours, and he's making do with the last plot on this side of the village. Well, he did insist on the brook, and jokes that it will be useful for drowning kittens in. He boasts that the stretch of land at the back of the house will become a fertile garden with vegetables, fruit and flowers – the lot.

You would be best served by staying in England. Life remains hard here. The English may be a little soft, but they can well afford to be. Aren't they as exhausted as we are? Let them rest – there is no harm in it, especially if you prosper, too.

Naturally, I miss you, although I wonder what Wittgenstein would make of such an unequivocal statement. I can be content enough if I am helping your parents to create a new home, knowing that at the appropriate time, you will also return to live in it. A word of warning to you, as well, though – please do not depend on my infallibility. I do not have all the answers, only (as I've heard) an 'awareness of the growth and dissolution of philosophical puzzlement,' and I suppose, the knowledge that I am, here, your beloved Rainer.

Luneburg. September 24th, 1947.

51

I was about to have a tooth pulled.

'Make sure you go to the toilet before we go,' my mother said, 'whatever you do, don't eat anything. The gas will mess up your insides.'

My first visit to the dentist had been quite interesting. Mr Cutler had a lamp in his waiting-room filled with blobs of red putty which floated around and made strange, elasticated shapes. My mother was angry when I told her that I could see the hairs up his nose when he was drilling. 'He's a member of the Rotary Club,' she said. 'Besides, your father's got clumps of the stuff coming out of his ears.' And then quietly, 'Poor devil.'

We walked past the Conservative Club on the way to Mr Cutler's. 'Just popping to the Co-op for some eclairs,' I was told, 'though you'd better not have one with your teeth.'

By the time we reached the supermarket, I was hungry. I took a small packet of 2d. KP Peanuts from a shelf, melted behind the canned vegetables and ate them all. My mother suddenly appeared round the cheese counter, and stared at the crumpled packet in my hand.

'Have you eaten those?'

I couldn't deny it.

'Right,' she said, and lifted me by the shirt-collar and bundled me out through the front doors of the supermarket on to the edge of the pavement.

'Bend over.'

I bent over.

'Open your mouth.'

I opened it.

'Tell me when it's all gone,' she said, and put three fingers down the back of my throat. The peanuts came up almost immediately.

She asked me if that was the lot, but thought she'd better have another go, just in case. 'I'm not letting that gas mess you up,' she said, 'wider now.'

By this time, a small crowd had gathered inside the Co-op, its faces pressed eagerly against the plate-glass window. My mother gave me 2d. when she'd finished.

'Go and tell the lady on the register what you did, and give her the money.'

I did as I was told.

The lady at the register had a label on her apron. It said 'Dorothy'.

'I took some peanuts and now I've come to pay for them,' I offered wildly.

'Never mind that – how's your throat, young man?' Dorothy said, but took the 2d. anyway.

I was only ten, but I felt I was growing up too quickly.

'I've got a man's head in a pair of girl's slacks,' I announced to my mother.

'Don't be daft,' she said, 'go and tidy your room.'

She had just made tomorrow morning's breakfast, and was busy putting the fuses back in the fuse box. Lately, she had taken to regulating the amount of light and heat we could use in the whole house by hiding all the fuses until she felt the time was right for a fire or light to be switched on. This was in addition to detaching the bath-plug from its thin chain and hiding it in the airing cupboard so that nobody could waste the hot water.

'Why can't we be like normal people?' I asked.

'Normal people don't have you and your father to waste electricity,' she said. Then she went on about how Nanna and Tatters had taken all the money from the business, and that since Uncle Dennis had lost the stock, things were very tight.

'Is that why I had to have these trousers?'

'I never had new trousers when I was your age.'

'You're a woman. Women don't wear trousers.'

'That's not the point. I've always had to make do. We spoil you enough as it is.'

I didn't feel spoilt.

'Can I have a dog?'

'Sure. And who would look after it. Me. No thank you.'

'Are we really poor?'

The magnitude of the question almost stopped my mother wiping the toaster.

'It depends what you mean. Not compared to some people.'

'Mrs Frings has got a spaniel. Does that make her richer than us?'

'Of course not.'

I knew that my mother had sold several of her rings in the last few months, and that Aunty Ruby had left the office. I'd already noticed how the jewellery my father was making looked inadequate compared to Tatters' grand designs in his sketch books.

The outside world was beginning to come into focus. It was within touching distance. I was beginning to suspect that my mother was right when she said that so many things weren't really worth remembering. Aunty Betty played some of her poetry to me: 'The childhood shows the man, As morning shows the day'. And I remembered Uncle Lance, and thought it might be the beginning of the end, except I didn't quite know what that meant.

Dear Rainer,

You dare moan that I should not depend on you. Your letters still give me comfort, in addition to the care and attention you continue to show towards Mama and Papa. Now what do you say? Don't go humble on me

Before going to sleep, I try to imagine what you all look like now, think how the house is coming on, even about that miserly old sod Hinrichs. Poor Heinz – he always used to pull my plaits and carry my satchel at school, and now he is a balding fatty. Time, no doubt, will get the better of us all before we know it. Then we'll be dead.

Your comments on Wittgenstein are just like you. So what if you say they have some practical use? How can I use them? I can't swallow everything. How can I begin to understand the Reverend Bacon's treatment of his wife? Maybe it is all relative. Then again, maybe I'm simply getting used to it. I dare say you wouldn't like that, because then I wouldn't be thinking.

Besides being a runty fart, Peter Slythe does have money, as my Reverend keeps telling me. He's very good at 'reminding' me about things. 'St Stephen's wouldn't be the church it is without the Slythe metal money.'

Of course, it turns out that the Reverend Bacon sucks up to a whole gang of businessmen around here. He's a slippery so-and-so. There was a large bridge party last night – another game I have to learn? – and the front room was full to bursting with manufacturers and retailers, not to mention the Bishop of Birmingham himself, who is very good at poker and whist, and plays the trombone. I gathered that the Reverend hopes to get a 'Stations of the Cross' series out of it all, but I'll be buggered if I know how.

I can put up with all this, Rainer, and (yes, yes) I understand what you say – but something still troubles my little mind. I can't quite put my finger on it – but only yesterday, Nicholas asked his father whether he believed in God.

'Haaaaaa – well, yes, there's a question. Of course I do,' stubbing his cigarette out.

'Why?' The boy was not to be put off. Bless him.

'Because I have a faith in His existence.'

'Is that all you need?'

'It is for me.'

'Does Allah exist?'

'What?'

'Allah – it's the Muslim name.' (We've been reading The Arabian Nights.)

'Yes, yes. I know.'

'Does He exist, though?'

'Not for me.'

'But for some people?'

'Rather large numbers of them I've been led to believe. Yes, I suppose so.'

'I don't want to believe in anything.'

'Oh dear. Don't you?'

'Not particularly.'

The Reverend paused. 'Well no one's going to force you, I don't suppose.'

You might as well have faith in Dulcie Slythe's fortune-telling cards. Or any cards. Or anything. So I understand what you say about Wittgenstein, but lines have to be drawn somewhere, don't they? I want to see Bacon being straight-forward about his beliefs, whatever they might be. Standing up for them. It's all so soggy. I'm sorry, egghead, but after all, it was you who helped me to respect the 'clarity and shape of ideas'; carpenter's bag of tools – my arse!

No doubt you see my agitation as a weakness, but I wouldn't mind. Any attention from such a cold fish is better than none.

Besides all that, I'll tell you about last Tuesday evening. I helped Mrs Bacon with the cooking for supper; there was a great deal of food. Somehow we'd got hold of pork loin, with peas, potatoes and rhubarb. I assumed there was going to be more than one guest and the usual lot would descend, locust-like. But only one man eventually turned up; Marcus Hull, (fifteen minutes late). He had a voice like a fog-horn. 'Naturally, I've left Cohen-Letts now. The City's attracting exactly the wrong kind of people. Who knows where the country's going and what will become of us all? All this austerity nonsense. How much will people wear it? I wonder: No – I thought South Africa might fill the bill nicely, especially whilst things settle down in Europe. The mining's pretty good, I hear. You ought to go, Bacon. Plenty of spin-offs for someone like you.' Talk about speaking through your arse.

The Reverend replied politely that he wasn't particularly

interested in missionary work. There followed a lengthy discussion about the prospects of striking it rich and the fluctuating price of gold. It emerged that Hull is great friends with the Bishop ('good old Hugo'), and that Bacon could become a Canon. He's obviously canvassing support, the old brown-nose.

During the meal, Hull's round face grew even fatter, and the sides of his glasses became embedded in the mound of flesh below his temples. He was quietly farting to himself all evening.

The conversation swung around to the creation of what they're calling the Welfare State. The act is due to be passed next year.

Inevitably, Hull put his oar in. 'Crying shame,' he said. 'People getting something for nothing.'

'Not quite for nothing, I don't think,' the Reverend Bacon whispered after a rather awkward silence. I was clearing the pudding away at this point – which I didn't like; rhubarb, like oranges, is too stringy.

'More or less for nothing. As near as dammit.' Hull's eyes were glowing, far away from the front of his face, like coals, but with no actual heat coming from them.

'Haaaa, well, yes – but people getting medical help, schooling, and so on.'

'That's not my point, Bacon. The point is, that it creates exactly the wrong sort of expectations.'

'I'm sorry . . .' wiping some custard from his mouth.

'If chaps think they can expect something for nothing,' and he fixed a squinty gaze on the Reverend and Mrs Bacon to make certain that there was no mistaking what he was about to say,'then where will we be? Answer me that.'

'Expect?'

'That's right. Expect.'

Mrs Bacon shot her husband a glance, and I started to fuss with the ashtrays. Nobody was actually smoking, but to hell with it, I thought. 'Everyone will be entitled to it,' she offered, softly but with a deliberate firmness.

'Says who?'

'The law.'

'The law's idiotic. Everybody knows that. Free milk! Before we know it, they'll be handing out cash to the needy!'

'Well – haaaaa! – I think that's on Mr Attlee's agenda, too.'

Hull ignored him. 'So it sounds very neat, but it won't work. All thinking men are agreed about that. Even that lot who've decided to be Socialists for the moment. The war's let in this kind of legislation – and I don't suppose Fascism has a very good name at the moment.' He smirked at his little joke, oblivious to me.

'I suppose I could do a sermon on it,' said the Reverend Bacon eagerly, making up for lost ground. But Hull was clearly hypnotised by the sound of his own voice.

'I suppose Slythe is delighted at all this scrap-metel he's got to deal with these days; I gather he took a bit of a knock in the slump. I should think Dulcie will stay with him now. I wouldn't have put money on it before . . .'

I scurried off into the kitchen and thought of Papa's teeth and your daily walk with the milk churn. I wondered how you would have felt about Marcus Hull. Is he a new game to be learnt? A new bag of tools to be sorted through?

. . . excuse me, dear Rainer, as I am finishing this letter in bed, and thinking fondly of you despite the outbursts. Goodnight.

Nr. Stratford. October 4th, 1947.

I was finding it difficult to sleep at nights. When I closed my eyes and opened them again, the room became long, thin and very narrow, like a tunnel. The window and the pink curtains seemed distant. Everything was still. Then, the material would slowly fold back, revealing a hand. Like a conjuror's hand, it was flat and stiff, showing both sides to me and inviting closer inspection. I never went closer, but I would watch for several long minutes before falling asleep.

– 3 –

Before going on to prep. school, I had been at Applefields nursery school for two years. We wore red enamel badges with apples on them. Aunty Betty saw Eden, but my time wasn't happy. I was sent home for not eating tomato soup, and had earned a reputation for unprovoked ferocity by biting Sarah Ford. For the afternoon sleep, my little red plastic bed was shoved a couple of yards away from the other children. I was not to be trusted.

My mother told me how much money Cedarhurst would cost her a few months before I arrived, but I restrained my guilt until the evening before the first term started.

'Why do you want me to go if it costs money?'

'Your grandparents said they'd pay. I'll believe it when I bloody see it.'

She passed me my night snack. The condensation was already forming on the unwrapped and pre-cut Milky Way, which had been lying around on a polystyrene tray for about six hours by this time.

'Has your father shown you how to do your tie yet?'

'No,' I replied.

'That's him all over. I'll do it.'

Monday nights, as a special treat, I usually watched *Z Cars* with my mother. There was a programme on the other side called *All Our Yesterdays*. Much as I liked Jock, and had already decided I wanted to be a policeman in a blue squad car when I grew up, I thought it looked interesting.

It showed old newsreel footage from the Second World War.

My mother was horrified.

'As if they haven't got anything better to show. Dredging up things like that.' She switched over, and must have seen my disappointment.

'Your father was at Dunkirk, you know. Mind you, they'd have been better off leaving him for all the good he did,' she cackled. 'Have a carrot.'

This was the second phase of the night snack – the wholesome, healthy part.

When she went to get a sherry in the middle of the programme, I was tempted to sneak a look at the other side, but decided it probably wasn't a good idea.

It wasn't.

My father took me to school the next morning. On the way, we played 'Spot the Mini'. He was very proud of his own Mini, and had worked out that if everybody drove small cars there would be much less congestion on the roads. He raced all the larger ones away from the traffic lights.

My father's Mini was no ordinary Mini; it had a statuette of a golfer on the bonnet, electric windows, a record player and a coffee percolator fixed to the walnut dashboard. 'Don't tell your mother about the record player, though,' he said to me, 'she thinks it's a heating system.' And then, by way of information, 'It cost a bit of money. Best she doesn't know.'

At school, I was often in trouble. Eventually, I had all my gold stars taken away for knocking on Mrs Cooper's door and then running away. She was pregnant, and I knew she could never get to the door quickly enough to see who it was.

I sneaked extra bottles of milk by climbing through the windows in the toilet to get to the crates in the alley outside. Once, however, I slipped, and Miss Littlehales had to pull my foot out of the lavatory bowl. Also, I'd been sick all over Mrs Hunter.

On the school trip to Dudley Zoo, I was left by myself in the Monkey House for behaving like one and making faces at the chimpanzee. I was stuck in there the whole day with a pack of my mother's gherkin and cress sandwiches.

We had to write an essay called 'My Parents'. Mrs Cheeseby was our teacher. She was old and very short with hair like wool, and had to stand on a chair to reach the top of the blackboard. Often, she would fall asleep in the middle of a sentence while she was reading to us. She looked mildly pleased but bored with our writing, though much of it was about gardening, golf, housework and grabbing forty winks in front of the television. I was sure that mine was more interesting, and shook with excitement as my turn appraoched to 'read out'.

'My father could have been a war hero, and my mother worked on the stage . . .'

Mrs Cheeseby was dozing, but a part of her seemed keen, and she nodded quietly to herself.

'My father was at Dunkirk. He left his rifle on the beaches and brought his cricket bat back instead.'

Mrs Cheeseby opened one eye and glanced around the room.

'But my mother thinks he should have stayed because he's no good at fighting. She was a stripper, but says she wouldn't show her bosoms if she could help it, although the feathers were a bit difficult to manage sometimes . . .'

Mrs Cheeseby woke up with a start; but the rest of the class were murmering approval, so I pushed on.

'Aunty Betty isn't to know, as Jesus, who lives near her potting shed, wouldn't understand. My mother is very kind to Aunty Betty, who is having trouble with her waterworks again at the moment. My mother says she's lucky, because Aunty Pam doesn't really have any waterworks left . . .'

'Stop!' called Mrs Cheeseby, in a hoarse whisper. 'Is it all like this?'

'What do you mean, Mrs Cheeseby?'

'What about housework – and such like?'

'That comes later . . . when my mum takes her clothes off.'

There was a silence. The waters were running deep and becoming rather too murky. Mrs Cheeseby collected the essays in and said she'd read mine more carefully later on. When I got home and told my mother about it, she said, 'I was only joking. I wasn't really a stripper. You'd better have a Milky Way.'

The headmaster of Cedarhurst was Mr Callaghan. He had been a major in the army, and now he had an E-type Jaguar and a glass eye. He smoked cigars and insisted that the boys raised their caps and the girls curtsied when they saw him looking out of his study window.

Mr Callaghan spoke to me twice during my first year at his school. Mrs Cheeseby's classroom was next to his office. For no reason, there was a large-scale map of Essex on the wall between the two rooms and a bookcase piled high with copies of *Macbeth* and *Tarka the Otter*. The school had managed to buy large quantities of each book cheaply, and next year we would have to do a book project comparing them.

I was always being sent out of the classroom. One day, Mr Callaghan stopped and asked me what I was doing.

'I've been sent out, Sir,' I said, rather obviously.

'What did you do then?'

'It wasn't my fault, Sir,' I blurted helplessly, and perhaps even more obviously. 'Jane Peat took my ruler and all I did was to ask for it back – except she wouldn't, so we had an argument and as I've got a louder voice, I was sent out.'

'I see,' said Mr Callaghan, as sagely as possible. He

leant over confidentially towards me. I could smell tobacco. 'Boys always get the thin end when they're dealing with girls. Remember that.'

'Thank you, Sir.'

'And try not to say anything next time. Give the culprit a look – a stare so terrifying that they'll give your ruler back immediately, and you won't get into trouble. You can't learn much out here.'

'Braintree, Sir.'

'Say it again.'

'Braintree.' I pointed to the map. 'I know if off by heart. I'll do Romford next week.'

'Give me your best stare,' he said.

'Like this, Sir?' I tensed my neck muscles and strained my head towards him, bulging one eye almost out of its socket and closing the other one with piratical concentration.

That's the ticket,' he said, and continued his walk along the corridor.

Later that year, we did a book project. We had to read a handful of books that we hadn't done at school, and write a report on them for the end of term. I kept mine secret, having done the research from my parents' bookshelf.

When Mrs Cheeseby had marked them, she handed the folders back with words of informed congratulation. Sally-Anne had done *Black Beauty* and *Animal Farm*; she was particularly commended for the 'lovely drawings'. Christopher Jenkins had done some

66

Famous Five books, which weren't very hard, but because we all knew there was something funny about Christopher, nothing was said.

Mrs Cheeseby was not a sophisticated or controversial person, and when it came to my project she said, 'I think Mr Callaghan would like to see you about this.'

So I found myself in the corridor outside his study once more.

Above the door were three lights: red, orange and green. After I'd knocked, the red one blinked on, quickly followed by the orange. It stayed that way for several minutes, so I pretended to be Nigel Boocock anxious to make the tapes at the start of a race. As I opened the throttle, the light turned to green and the door opened.

'I'd like to see you for a minute,' Mr Callaghan said, 'come in.'

I pretended to adjust my tie like I'd seen Uncle Dennis doing, and went inside.

Mr Callaghan lit a cigar and looked at me with his good eye.

'Your project seems very . . .', he puffed enthusiastically, '. . . grown-up. Very adult.'

'The books I used *were* grown-up,' I replied proudly, with disarming dramatic emphasis.

'Do you normally read those kinds of books at home?'

'Sometimes. But I've read *One Hundred and One Dalmatians* as well,' I said, hopefully.

He came to the point. 'Imprisonment. Mutilation. Violence. Why have you written about these things?'

I took a deep breath, but didn't let it out immediately.

At home, I had found *Mein Kampf*, the five-volume *Illustrated History of the Second World War* and a novel about black slavery which my mother was reading. I had sneaked a look at this, and asked why black people were so badly treated. She told me that was the way things were when the book was written. I asked if it was the same as the Jews I'd read about in the illustrated history. She told me it was the work of a few cruel people who told everyone else what to do. She had shown me photographs of herself as a young girl in the Hitler Youth, and drawn a picture of the uniform she'd had to wear. Her father had been in the secret police, though she said he didn't know about the Jews. They all loved Hitler, because nobody had anything to eat in Germany before he came along. They didn't believe the things that were said about him in England. My mother and I decided that once people had chosen to like or dislike something, it was very difficult to change their minds. She said people were too obsessed with 'fads'. We drew up a list of people we knew who were stuck on particular ideas – Aunty Betty with her God, my father with his Minis and electrical gadgets, and Mrs Frings with people in white coats watching her. (This wasn't the moment to talk about fuses or housework.) People were very resistant to change. I put all this into my project, and called it, 'What People Will Accept', and said that Hitler had thought about it in prison. My mother thought he was strange because he was insecure and only had one testicle, and really wanted to father everyone.

But how could I begin to tell Mr Callaghan all this?

'Why didn't you choose something more . . . appropriate?' he urged.

I wanted to say that it was because it didn't interest me, but, instead I said, 'I don't know. I'm sorry, Sir.'

When I told my mother, she took me to Pattison's for a custard tart and a banana milkshake. I still didn't understand what was wrong with my project.

'People are afraid of the truth,' she said. 'There's no need to ram it down their throats, though.' She put some red lipstick on, smacked her lips together and undid another button of her blouse. 'Come on. We're off to the library.'

I valued my mother's eccentric intensity. She lived her life honestly, if not fully, and I found security in her bizarre certainties.

She said, 'Find yourself a friend and I'll buy you a pair of trousers with a zip.'

At times like that, I believed in her without question.

I should confess that your talk of a Welfare State and Marcus Hull touches some kind of nerve in me. Would that we even had a State to call our own.

Forgive me. We have been subject to a certain amount of anxiety over the past two weeks. I should enlighten you . . .

There are strong suggestions that some of our so-called neighbours have been attempting to find evidence that would reclassify your father – there is plenty of money to be made here, 'bad blood' money. I think Hinrichs is in the clear, but there are indications that Kugler – the new baker – and Mittelstadt are involved. Your father is happy enough to be catalogued as a 'Follower of Nazism' (indeed, how many of us can deny it? Question: at what point does an initial and passive adherence to a set of ideals, later regulated through fear and confusion, become a conscious, wilful choice?), and I suppose his army days will never allow him to become completely 'Exonerated'. But think of the consequences if he becomes a 'Lesser Offender' or – as some are suggesting – a 'Major Offender'. It won't just be the job at the brick factory that he'll be worrying about then.

In Hitzacker (only fifteen kilometres or so downriver; after all), they denounced a man and tried to string him up – on the spot. The Allies, the MP, arrived barely in time, but, overall, it turns out that they are having great difficulty separating the sheep from the goats. Doubtless quotas have been allocated – they must be seen to be doing something.

People are speculating about your father, as his captors did three years ago, but I doubt that anybody can act on mere suspicion, even in this atmosphere. It's a delicate matter, and best not discussed in these pages. My belief is that the whole business will blow itself out as quickly as it began, and the Allies will realise the futility of such an operation. In the meantime, be assured that I will keep your father's head down. Trust me.

You can't blame people for trying to survive, even at others' expense. Those 40 DMs, that were given to us all for 'fresh starts' are all very well – but, for most, they have disappeared quickly, even if for a few the amount has been multiplied a thousandfold. Russian watchtowers ensure that we will never contemplate Communism, but we are now divided by wealth, by circumstance and by Fate – and are nervous of each other.

A short letter, and a bad-tempered one. Again, I apologise and ask you to be calm about your family and remember that (despite everything else) I am your beloved Rainer.

Luneburg. October 18th, 1947.

Once upon a time, a man travelled from one country to another. In his first land, he had been a duke, and was surrounded by admirers and grew accustomed to living in luxury.

A fortune-teller had told him not to take sides in a bitter war which was being fought amongst his own people, but he was a proud man, and ignored the warning. As a consequence, he lost all his lands and goods, and barely escaped with his life.

This man had a son, who was short of stature because – it was thought – of a curse that the fortune-teller had put on him for his disastrous pride.

Feeling guilty about his behaviour, and worried about his son, the duke filled his head with extravagant and fantastic stories about the wealth and the servants the family had left behind.

The son worked hard, and became a clockmaker. He was happy enough, and gained a reputation as a fine craftsman, although his father's stories never left his head. He developed a weakness for fine clothes and ate lavishly whenever he could afford it.

Eventually, the time came for him to marry, and he fell in love with two sisters. However, not knowing which one to choose, he went to his father – now an old man – for advice.

The bent figure called his son close to him and hissed that to make a decision, he must ask both sisters how they would make him happy.

So the clockmaker went to the first sister and said, 'I will provide you with everything you need, but how will you make me happy?'

And she replied, 'I love you dearly, but don't yet know how to make you happy. I will love you with all my heart, and trust that this will be enough.'

The young man nodded his approval at this. He went to see the second sister, and said, 'I will provide you with everything you need, but how will you make me happy?'

And she replied, 'I will love you dearly,' and then flattered him by praising the clothes he wore and the exquisite meals she had often seen him eating.

This greatly pleased the clockmaker, and he chose to marry the second sister.

As the two grew old together, he prospered and grew wealthy; but as quickly as he could make money, so his wife would spend it.

As his resources ebbed away, he tried to tell his wife, but his pride would never let him admit how bad the situation was really becoming. She would only say, 'But you have a beautiful silver-topped cane and I have a wonderful collection of hats. What could be wrong?'

He wondered whether he should deceive his wife about the money that he made, but she watched him like a vulture, and he was not a man who liked an argument.

The clockmaker grew wretched, but was still not inclined to speak against his wife.

He began to remember the time when he was happy, yet even its vague memory saddened him.

He was surrounded by the clocks he had collected over the years, all ticking on, unwinding Time, reminding him that his memories were only that.

He wished that his head hadn't been so full of his father's exotic words, and that he'd listened to the first of the two sisters, who was now married to a marma-lade maker and lived in a cottage amongst rows of neatly trimmed orange trees.

The clocks ticked on, and chimed cruelly every hour.

The son began to collect items to remind himself of happier times. He took to hiding these from his wife, in case she guessed at his reasons and became angry.

When he died, she found bags of toffee stuffed behind cushions. She discovered pages of poetry writ-ten in an elegant hand hidden underneath the carpet. She came upon unopened bottles of stout wedged behind clothes in the wardrobe.

She threw the toffees away, burnt the poetry and poured the stout down the sink. She told everyone that in his old age, her husband had become a little crazy.

The clocks ticked on.

One night, instead of chiming midnight at the same time, the clocks struck one after the other. As soon as one had finished, the next would strike up, and so on.

The house echoed to the sounds of the bells, which chased each other round the rooms and clambered up the stairs towards the room where the clockmaker's wife was asleep.

The sound was deafening, and she woke up with a start.

Then the chiming ceased, and all the clocks stopped ticking, forever.

All of a sudden, I started to get the hang of school. I began to win prizes, all for English – spelling, dictation, stories and letter writing. We weren't allowed to choose, and I was given a book on the Antarctic, a novel about a gang of thieves who stole pillar boxes and, the only one I read, the story of *The Golden Fleece*.

'Your father's written a book,' my mother said, by way of congratulation.

I looked impressed, and she added: 'It's called, *British Speedway Averages and Aggregates – 1953/4.*'

I was still quite impressed.

'But nothing like this lot.' She tapped the letter from Mr Callaghan and folded it into the calendar.

'Did you ever write anything?' I asked.

'I was always too busy for that kind of thing. A few letters,' she added reluctantly, 'but that was all. Tatters once wrote a play. He was very keen on amateur dramatics.'

The only play I'd ever seen was *Mother Goose* last Christmas. I hadn't liked it. The humour had seemed very obvious, but the parents had laughed uncontrollably, whilst their children only shuffled about and looked bored. I tried to show an interest.

'Did Tatters act as well?'

'You'll have to ask your father. I think he got fed up with playing small men. He is quite stunted, you know.'

I wondered where Tatters' play was, and I thought of him never having the chance to be a dashing lead, but always the cheery short one who's there to add humour to the plot and make everyone else look better.

I told my mother.

'He's all right. Anyway, they've got bags of money.' Then she rummaged in her white handbag, and drew out a bar of pale, cracked chocolate. It had been in there for several days, and was no longer in its original wrapper. Instead, it was covered with the plastic bag the carrots had come in the week before.

'Thanks,' I tried.

'And don't make crumbs. I've only just done the floors.'

Along with the prizes came a new sort of respect from the teachers. From the lower reaches of Door Monitor, I bypassed 'Chalk' and 'Milk' and 'Flower', and

75

went straight to Bell Ringer. Every Wednesday, someone from our class had to ring the bell to end school for the day. There were two bells standing in the small alcove on the landing, and the first time I chose the wrong one – but Mrs Cheeseby didn't say anything. I knew that some kind of plateau had been reached.

I still don't have a proper pair of trousers. Auntie Claire and Uncle Frank had taken Simon, the first friend I'd ever had, to Coventry. Since then, I had only had two friends, and my mother didn't approve of either of them.

Paul Wertheim was nineteen years old, but, due to an accident on a building site, had a mental age of ten.

'That boy's got a metal plate in his head,' she said. 'You've got to be careful with that sort.'

However, I thought Paul was a rare find. He was very bulky, with thick-lensed glasses, and his parents owned twenty-four dalmatians. He could play the first few chords of 'House of the Rising Sun' on his electric guitar, and allowed me to look at his rude magazines.

Murray Winterholme was near my own age, but still older. My mother was deeply suspicious.

'You know why he's called Winterholme don't you?'

I didn't.

'It used to be Winterbottom, but they changed it. Winter – *bottom*.'

Paul, Murray and I used to play British Bulldog on the patch of green opposite our house. With only three

76

it wasn't much fun and, as I was the youngest, I would never win. When they caught me, Paul and Murray would make a great show of pinning me to the ground. My mother could see everything from the kitchen window, her mostly naked form moving methodically about behind the blinds, blurred but watchful.

'I was on the telephone to Betty,' she lied. 'I saw you with Paul and Murray.'

'It was British Bulldog,' I said. 'They always win, but I don't mind.'

'I bet you don't. Don't let things get out of hand, though.'

I didn't know what she meant. There was an uncomfortable silence. She poured a sherry and looked for something to wipe.

'Be careful of that Paul. He's got manly urges – but he's not quite all there. He's not under full control.'

I looked confused.

'I've said enough. Just don't let him get his hands on your doofers.'

I knew that my mother and father married, lived together and had me. I also knew that their mothers and fathers had done more or less the same thing. In *Thunderball*, James Bond got his girl though he didn't marry her and there weren't any children. I knew that some people lived together, but weren't married. I knew that when my mother said 'doofers' it was because she didn't want to talk about something.

In fact, Paul – and sometimes Murray – did try to get their hands between my legs, but I couldn't tell my mother. I asked her what she meant.

'Homos,' was all she'd tell me. 'Men shouldn't be with other men. Passion's all right, but in its place. Ask your father.'

I buried myself in *The Golden Fleece*. Jason did have the Argonauts, but they all seemed so involved with finding the Fleece. Maybe the story was being deliberately evasive, but then it would have lost its momentum. 'Tiphys the helmsman' and 'Lyceneus, whose sight was preternaturally keen' seemed to be too distracted by what was happening in Lemnos, Cios and Colchis to be bothered with each others' doofers.

For the moment, I stopped playing British Bulldog with Paul and Murray. My mother bought me a tennis ball, and we played Hot Rice, which involved throwing the ball as hard and as often as possible at me.

'Look,' I said to her, pulling down my striped riding slacks and exposing my thighs. There were seven or eight blue-black bruises luridly tattooed on them.

'They're only having fun,' she smiled, and broke open a packet of Penguins.

Rainer – I am worried about Papa. He can be an idiot. Make sure the silly sod doesn't land himself in it. I don't think the Allies can sustain a witch hunt. Maybe I still have faith in the other villagers. Despite his blustering, they are still his friends. Really, there's nothing I can do. Once again, I have to depend on you.

78

*I am sending you one of the Reverend's old overcoats —
winter is approaching and an unfinished house will not give
you much warmth. In addition to some tins of food (tongue
again). Use them. If it's any consolation, things aren't much
better over here; people are already complaining of the cold,
and worried about damaged pipes. Everyone is sick to the
back teeth of austerity.*

*Perhaps I should feel guilty about this, but I cannot — and
will not. For me, compassion and guilt have become separate.
I know which side my bread is buttered, and even if Mrs
Bacon should only have a single powdered egg to boil for the
old Reverend, I should still send you everything I could lay
my hands on rather than help her. That's the way it is.*

*Sometimes I feel the English are getting what they
deserve. There is no belief, no love, no anger, no malice,
little purpose. No vision. Nothing of consequence. Everything is worn out.*

*It's mainly the men — Mrs Bacon is different. She worked
as a nurse and went to Normandy in 1944. She remembers
the dying, and all the rest of it. She told me the soldiers were
always very quiet; they seemed to feel that the less said, the
better. No impassioned calls to God, or fevered memories of
home. She particularly remembers one young sergeant trying
to write a letter to his parents telling them that his brother,
their son, had been killed. He couldn't do it; he tried several
times and eventually started to cry before falling asleep.
When he woke up, he tore up his efforts, and wrote a letter
which didn't even mention his brother.*

*A funny lot. I feel differently about them, now. There is
nothing to really offend or inspire.*

*The Reverend Bacon is a difficult man to talk with,
although after a drink or two even he'll hold forth about his*

time in Burma. Peter Slythe doesn't need the drink, but he takes it anyway. He gets verbal diarrhoea about his war years, almost proud of them, in fact. He told me that 'the slump had done for me. The war coming along when it did was a stroke of luck. Never looked back since.'

He talks of Egypt, and drinking two whole bottles of 'the local drink' in one night, by himself. Most people were drunk for a lot of the time, he says – especially the Americans – mainly to overcome fear, blot out the prospect of death, overcome boredom, whatever. He said I should know about these things because the English could usually smell schnapps in the German ranks. If there was no odour, the English would be more confident.

Yesterday, after a few of Reverend Bacon's whiskies, Peter Slythe rolled into the kitchen where I was, as usual, doing the washing-up.

'You don't know what it was like.'

'Don't I?'

'From a man's point of view?'

He moved closer. I could smell the alcohol on him. Soused.

'We were lonely. Do you understand what I mean?' I nodded.

'The front line was the most Godforsaken, sexless place on earth. We were constantly teased, reminded of our needs' – 'Jane' in the Daily Mirror, Lana Turner showing her tits, especially in Ziegfeld Girl.

> 'I love you in your negligee
> I love you in your nightie
> But when the moonlight flits
> across your tits –
> By Christ all-fucking mighty!'

By this time, Slythe was swaying, occasionally using the table to support himself. I stared straight ahead, massaging an imaginary stain out of the gravy boat. After a couple of refrains, he shushed himself, and admitted that on VE Day, when Jane stripped off for the first time (after all those years of provocative promise!), 'I wasn't even sure what to think or do. I'd been led this dance by a cartoon strip for years, and now she'd done what I wanted her to do . . . I don't know . . . all that desire . . . no outlet.' He told me that getting VD was a punishable offence. 'Remember, flies spread diseases. Keep yours shut!' Do you know what greasy Bacon said to me the other day? 'The good thing about the war was that individuals didn't matter. There were only men.' The old goat.

I have decided to send you a hat, and some English newspapers.

Nr. Stratford. November 2nd, 1947.

It was the end of the Spring term, rain was tearing across the sky. Mr Callaghan was a man who thought holidays ought to be earned; before Christmas, he had made the whole school listen to Beethoven's Fifth Symphony. It had taken the entire afternoon, but, as it meant missing Algebra with Mr Bulmer, I didn't mind. He was a large, angular man who was always wheezing and looked very old. He had white hair and a purple face with red lines mapping their way across a huge rock of a nose.

Now we were all sitting in the dining hall with blank pieces of papers and pencils. We weren't allowed home until we'd drawn a diagram of all the fielding positions on a cricket field.

'This is the mark of a civilised upbringing,' Mr Callaghan had cheerfully informed us. It was still raining outside, and I thought of my mother waiting outside with the spring-loaded umbrella. I'd broken it a few days ago, but hadn't got round to telling her.

I put two crosses on the paper and wrote 'wicket-keeper' and 'bowler' by them. I knew where the slips should be, but how many were there? I decided on four, and sprayed them out to the wicket-keeper's right. I fielded at mid-on or mid-off because I couldn't throw properly ('Just like your father'), so filled them in, too.

The boy next to me had almost finished. He had brought his own pen, the kind that allowed you to change the colour of the ball-point at the click of a plastic button. He was putting his cross in red, writing in green and underlining in black. The stumps were a kind of pink. I looked disconsolately at my stubby pencil.

'Could I have a go?' I asked.

'It's got thirteen different colours.' He passed the pen over. There was a heavy silence as he looked on expectantly.

'You don't know where silly-mid-on is, do you?' I said.

He opened the palm of his hand. I could see all the positions you could ever want, written in tiny but distinct print. I copied them down, deliberately getting mid-wicket and cover the wrong way round to avoid suspicion.

His name was Mark Perkins. We talked for a few minutes after handing the papers in. Could this be a friend? I split a Milky Way with him.

'My dad said I looked like the back of a bus when I was born,' I said extravagantly. 'And I had jaundice.'

He was as thin and shapeless as a pipe-cleaner. 'I've got asthma,' he replied imperiously, and let me touch his inhaler.

I invited him to lunch the next day, and asked him whether there was anything he couldn't eat as he was so ill. 'Mushrooms and eggs,' he said, and went to catch the bus back to Dorridge.

My mother was keen on the idea. 'Got yourself a little friend, have you?' she said, and gave Mark a plate of mushrooms on toast for tea. He ate half, then said he was full.

'Well, you're only a little chap. Not like mine – he's got hollow legs.'

I met Mark several more times during the Easter holidays. We played football together, and I ripped my slacks. He formed a secret club called the Secret Eye Detectives, and made me Deputy President. We had battles against a rival society which had been formed by Terry Morgan, whose father ran the news-agent's shop.

My mother seemed to approve, or else she was just relieved. As far as she was concerned, The Rolling Stones, cigarettes and homos had been encountered and repulsed. She bought me a new pair of skating boots and paid for five lessons at the local ice-rink. By the end of the holidays, I had been awarded a certificate for skating backwards.

My father's business was gradually recovering from the theft out of Uncle Dennis' Humber. With Tatters confined at home, he felt a new confidence and created another company, Paradise Investments. Tatters was dismayed at what was being sold, and continued to send him complex, fantastic designs for jewellery which would never get made.

My father bought a Mini for my mother and the house was suddenly overwhelmed with electrical gadgets – toasters, a five-inch television set, three radio-cassette recorders and an ice-cream maker. He also started to cultivate mushrooms in the cupboard under the stairs.

'What does he want all that stuff for?' Tatters said to me, although he had two televisions himself.

Mr Frings had bought Mrs Frings a radio-cassette player to help her through the days, and she recorded the disc-jockeys' comments between records, carefully leaving out the songs themselves.

'Just smile if she plays you something,' my mother said.

The tape revolution didn't help Aunty Betty either.

'I miss the sense of ritual you used to get with the spools,' she told us during a performance of Herbert's 'At the Church Door'. 'If God had intended it all to be so easy, he wouldn't have invented proper tape recorders.'

The world was going crazy. My mother bought a miniskirt and we had a red telephone installed in the kitchen. 'That'll bring a touch of class to the place,' she said fondly. 'You can't beat a good quality plastic.'

At school, most of the summer term was spent on a Time project. My recent high standing was immediately strained by this. I had two experts to help me, both called Andrew. One had a round red face and came to fix the electrics and drink my mother's sherry, and one was Uncle Lance's son, who was small like his father and at university.

I split the project into chapters. The first one was very conventional: clocks, the various time zones of the world shaded in different colours and a line pointing backwards to when time started. Along the line were plotted important dates and events, such as Adam and Eve, dinosaurs, the Plague and the Great Fire of London.

Both Andrews thought this was rather tame. Chapter Two was more ambitious, and explained how modern science had shown that there wasn't anything that could be called 'absolute time'. I stuck a picture of Einstein down and drew a diagram showing how one person in a spaceship would age at a different rate to his twin brother left on earth. 'Time is therefore relative to your situation and place,' I wrote.

Red-faced Andrew helped me to build a model of our galaxy and the Milky Way, using ping-pong balls and stars from the Christmas tree. Everything was held together by glue and coloured pipe-cleaners, and a chart showed how long it took light to reach us from other planets and stars.

But the third chapter ruined me.

I did some research in the *Encyclopaedia Britannica*, the set that a Canadian door-to-door salesman had sold to my father the night he'd proposed to my mother. 'He was excited. He just went berserk,' she told me.

It explained that the universe was created by a Big Bang, and how our planet was like a splinter from a huge explosion. I proudly drew my conclusions, and asked how we could measure Time if we weren't really sure where to start measuring from. I put some marbles in a balloon, and wrote tiny labels on them of each of the planets. Then I blew the balloon up, tied it and wrote around the outside, 'The Universe/Milky Way – please shake and pop for the beginning of Time.'

I wrote on the last page of the project, 'These discoveries about the start of the universe have thrown doubt on the existence of God himself!!'

'You'll be joining that Hari-Krishna lot before you know it,' my mother said. 'Best not to show it to Aunty Betty. Her toe's gone septic.'

At school, Mrs Cheeseby gave me a startled look and disappeared to see Mr Ross, next door but one. I was never asked to ring the bell again, and the flow of prizes dried up. The best Time project featured a papier-mâché cuckoo-clock, and a prayer was said in assembly for 'unbelievers everywhere'.

My mother said, 'You'll get used to it. That's the way it is.'

She was strange but she she was mostly on my side. I thought back to the project; maybe she'd have been more suited to another time and place. I imagined her face pressed against the inside of the balloon before being exploded to distant parts of the galaxy.

At the weekend, I told Nanna and Tatters about my difficulties at school. Nanna offered to warm some ice-cream up for me, and Tatters took me upstairs into his study. He told me that before he'd designed jewellery, he had been a keen reader of poetry. It felt as if something important was being revealed, and I listened carefully.

'No one listens to ideas they don't understand,' he said. He went to a white safe which stood partially hidden beneath a lace tablecloth in the corner of the room. The key was kept underneath the cloth. Tatters opened the safe and took out a small pile of old books. He told me about Kipling and Houseman, but said his favourite was Hardy, who had more than twenty cats and dogs buried in his back garden.

Hardy, he said, knew about the important of Time, how it changed things, and why it was so endless to the young but almost non-existent to the old. I wasn't sure if that was quite what I meant, but told him about the ping-pong balls and the balloon with marbles in it.

'What seems certain for some people,' he said, 'may well be different for others.' I thought of God out by

the potting shed, the doctors in Mrs Frings' hedge and
Nanna downstairs toasting the raspberry ripple.

'If you think about something long enough, it will
often be that way.' He took his glasses off, pointed to
his head and whispered, 'It's all in the mind.' Then he
read 'The Clock-Winder':

> 'Up, up from the ground
> Around and around
> In the turret stair
> He clambers, to where
> The wheelwork is
> With its tick, click, whizz
> Reposefully measuring
> Each day to its end
> That mortal men spend
> In sorrowing and pleasuring.
> Nightly thus does he climb
> To the trackway of Time.'

Tatters showed me his old stamp collection with the
heads of unfamiliar kings on the stamps, and told me
not to mind the teachers. My confidence recovered,
he put the books back in the safe. I looked inside as
the door swung slowly closed. I saw a pile of letters
and a few books. The door thumped against the thick
metal frame, was locked, and the key returned to its
resting place.

A pile of letters.

I cycled home along the footpath next to the golf
course, wondering about them.

When I arrived, my mother was very mysterious
and told me to wait outside the kitchen for a few

moments. I could hear her muttering and moving around. At last, she pushed the door open.

'That was a real sod.'

She put a small parcel of newspaper on the table.

'What is it?' I asked.

'You'd better not open it. That growth on the side of your bloody hamster got worse. The vet wasn't open. I had to do something or it would have burst.'

I looked appalled.

'I put it in the oven. As a kindness. It took more gas than I thought. Tough little bugger wasn't she?'

My dear, your letter arrived earlier today. I feel the need to reply immediately. Once again, you seem intent on picking at nerve-endings. Have patience with my response.

Do you remember that argument between Einstein and the two scientists Bohr and Heisenberg? Before Einstein went to America and attempted to prove that their Complementarity and Uncertainty Principles were incomplete – in particular, the proposition that an event cannot be said to exist until it is actually observed, and that before this, it is only a matter of potentialities. I have been reading a paper, courtesy of the British army and my lieutenant, by a man called Schrödinger who supports Einstein in his claims against these two. He made an experiment with a cat inside a box.

To cut a long story short, an experiment was set up so that the cat had an absolutely equal chance of living or being killed by gas fumes. According to the theories of Bohr and Heisenberg, the possibilities of life and death existed simultaneously in the box, and only when an observer opened it could one or other of them be said to have really existed. In other words, only by actually opening the box and seeing the cat could it actually be said to be alive or dead – up until that point, it was both – or neither! Schrödinger tried to show how ludicrous this notion was; the cat would be either alive or dead completely disregarding the presence of an observer. Now doesn't that make sense?

My point is this: there should be a more detached way of perceiving the world and the English, other than one which is so destructively dependent upon you as their sole observer.

There may well be something in what you say, but your letter already admits that our own troops were drunk on schnapps in the same way the English and the Americans were. And aren't we shattered and disheartened in the same ways? Do not sentimentalise such extreme misery and shape it into backbone and purpose; we have no choice and can only move in one direction – no, must move in order to survive.

Compare this to a (now) rare visit from Captain Fitzgerald three days ago. He said that he was going home to America, and although he brought some food, there was contempt in his voice. The food was wrapped up in the pages of an American magazine. After he'd gone, I looked at it. The front cover showed a scene, apparently from a story insde. Two girls were torturing (or was it tormenting?) a GI who was chained to a chair. He was handsome, obviously concealing fear in a defiant, admirable manner. One of the girls, dressed in a tight blouse and shorts, a blonde, was playing a blowtorch over his chest. The other girl was looking on, with a whip in her hand, an expression halfway between a snarl and a satisfied grin. The first girl shouted, 'Scream for mercy, Amerikaner Soldat!' Both of the girls were wearing aspects of Nazi uniform – caps, jackets, swastika armband, and so on.

What are we to make of that? Doubtless the jilted captain Fitzgerald was making his small point, but no matter – he has flown. But is the image of the American soldier and the German girls 'real', to him, in any way at all? The captain might think so. Think of the cat in the box and put yourself in its position. Is my meaning clear?

Now I must curse myself for raising such pandemonium. The reclassification scare has subsided, and I don't believe there will be any more worries. The Allies are finding it impossible and, as time moves forward, I am certain that – like you – we shall be 'exonerated', bureaucratically and by common consent.

Some good news – your father has a job at the brick factory. It will involve shift work, and he will be away two or three nights a week. Only watchman, but something.

Thank you for the newspapers – but the hat, alas, is on the small side. Never mind; I am certain that a use will suggest itself before long. In the meantime, I remain your beloved Rainer.

Luneburg. November 13th, 1947.

— 4 —

We all feel Time reversing hard past us. It leaves us in front but unwilling to move forwards. We may well live in a continuous present, not being able to 'see' Time slipping by, but we feel it, like the brush of a stranger's hand in a crowded railway station. We half turn, but the stranger is quickly lost to us. It could be anyone. It has been said that to think about Time is to acknowledge that our outward lives are controlled by clocks, whilst our inward lives are governed by the imagination, which knows no boundaries and cuts through mechanical notions of Time.

But this is not true.

Our inward lives are also governed by clocks . . . days, weeks, seasons and years. And death. Close our eyes and the stranger still brushes past.

Scientists tell us that there is no theoretical difference between forward and backward Time. In reality, though, we know the past but cannot remember the future. The inward life may be able to ignore boundaries, but it cannot go where it is not meant to. Really, it can only travel into the past, even whilst it is pushing cautiously into the future.

We *feel* that Time is passing. We know that increasing disorder is a sign that Time is moving forward. Everything starts from a position of order and moves towards chaos.

But inward Time is a personal concept, not an absolute one. It is relative to whoever is observing or measuring it and lags slightly behind the outward life's involuntary progress. It is like a damaged leg unable to quite catch its twin, forever aware of it moving slightly ahead.

Because the inward life can't see beyond the present, and because it can ignore boundaries, it travels backwards.

The inward life exists in a continuous and expanding past that never quite catches the present.

That past is never absolute.

It can never be shared.

It is uniquely personal.

The near-present and the past exist only in our minds, but the future doesn't exist at all. Not really. Not beyond science. Not even empty space or blurred lights up ahead. The stranger is always moving in the opposite direction to us.

It was summer, and as usual we went to Germany to see Opa, my mother's father. We always drove there in two Minis, leaving at what my mother called 'the crack of dawn', and travelling to Tilbury Docks where we caught a cargo ship – the *Doric Ferry* – to some-where called the Hook of Holland.

'That's it,' my mother shouted into the gloom. 'I'm not going. It won't be worth it at this rate.' We hadn't even started the journey. My father appeared on the drive, tamely clutching a small pink vanity case.

'What the hell have you got that one for?'

'You told me to bring it.'

'Not that one. The other one. With the talc and the Estée Lauder in it.' My mother always did herself proud when she went back to Germany.

My father stared blankly into the gloomy morning air before disappearing back up the drive and into the house again.

My mother's Mini was finally loaded with enough clothes and possessions to keep us going for eight weeks, although my father usually returned after two, 'to run the business'.

One year, for the first time, she had broken with habit and taken a different car. It was a grey Austin Maxi, built like a large box.

'Plenty of room in this,' she had gloated. 'If your father thinks he's getting me to Germany in that Mini again, he's got another think coming.'

To celebrate, she bought a small toy monkey and hung it on the rear-view mirror.

When we were driving through Germany she realised there was something strange about the new car. Villagers stared at it and men working on the road came half to attention as we made our way through the countryside. In one small town, a crowd gathered round the Maxi.

My mother inspected the car.

'They think we're the Chancellor,' she eventually said.

'Why?' I asked.

'Number plates. Silly sods.'

The registration contained the letters 'BON'. English plates also seemed more stately than the usual German ones.

My mother bought a white and black pennant with the German eagle on it. I recognised it as the same design I'd seen on the German footballers' shirts in the World Cup Final. My mother said its hooked beak reminded her of Nanna, and fixed it on to the front of the car. This emphasised the deception, though she continued to look straight ahead, a faint smile on her face, never acknowledging the eyes that invariably turned towards us.

One bright day, she put her hand up to shield her eyes from the sun's glare. A small group of men repairing a bridge snapped fully to attention and returned a smart military salute.

After that, she tried to persuade me to wear my *Z Cars* police cap and sit on a cushion, pretending to be a chauffeur.

Commanding such attention and being allowed right of way, she also came to love the car for its cavernous simplicity. It didn't have a radio, and there was plenty of room on the dashboard tray for moist scented tissues, lipsticks and jelly babies.

Back in England, my father had borrowed it for a business trip and written it off just outside Hemel Hempstead. He went to hospital for a week. After my mother had visited him, she said, 'At least the mon-key's all right.'

Now she found herself in a Mini again, overloaded with glass jars and luggage. At the quayside, the small cars were hauled into the bowels of the *Doric Ferry* in two bulging nets, which swung dangerously one hundred feet above our heads before being lowered to safety.

The crossing was rough, and my mother and I went on deck at night as the swelling sea was making it impossible to sleep in the cabin.

'You shouldn't have had those scrambled eggs,' she said. 'It looks like sick before you've even started.' There were six nuns on deck with us, also looking pale. 'Aunty Betty would love this.'

The nuns had all closed their eyes, although their hands gripped the rail tightly. They were rejoicing in the Lord, and thanking Him for their safe passage.

'We haven't got there yet,' my mother shouted above the wind. She gestured towards them. 'I bet you're glad you've got your scarves so well fixed. I nearly lost mine then.'

The nearest nun managed a pallid smile.

We stood silently together for about half an hour, staring into the rain, picking out small specks of light every now and then. My mother turned to me and said, 'We'd better find those mints before your father finishes the lot,' and we went down to the cabin again.

★

The drive from Holland to my grandfather's house took almost a day. We arrived late at night. I knew we were getting close because the roads were suddenly cobblestoned, rather than the smooth tarmac of the main highways. Opa lived in the middle of the countryside, and we passed through a tiny hamlet called Tostaglope. I was in my father's Mini, and at this point he always made the same joke.

'I wonder what's on at the Tostaglope Odeon tonight?' or 'Who are Tostaglope City playing in the cup?'

Tostaglope was the only German word he could successfully pronounce; 'Toaster-glope-ahh'.

I told my mother the joke the next morning.

'I don't think there's a cinema in Tostaglope,' she said, 'it's only a farmhouse and a barn.'

Opa had lived with a housekeeper called Elspeth since Oma keeled over and died. I could remember my grandmother as a severe but kind woman. She used to give me salt sticks whenever my mother told me I couldn't have any. Quite suddenly, whilst cycling into the village to buy some applecake, she'd had a heart attack. She was only fifty-nine. When the family had telephoned my mother in England to tell her the news, she'd howled loudly and startled me. I'd fallen over and cut my head open on the tiled kitchen floor. She said I hadn't cried so much since I'd had my stomach pumped after swallowing half a dozen mothballs the year before. The week after Oma died, we had yellow lino put down in the kitchen.

The first thing Opa did when it was daylight was to show us his garden. The grey, metal gate was padlocked, 'TO KEEP THE FLIES OUT,' he told me. He showed us neat rows of carrots, peas, stawberries, potatoes and beans. The sandy path through the middle was punctuated by black mole traps. Winding, semi-raised tunnels of earth came to an abrupt halt underneath two of them. Opa made a pinching motion with two fingers and smiled. My mother told me to stop looking shifty. I spoke to her in English and said I was thinking about the moles.

'Vermin,' she said. 'He's not out the garden and they're at his potatoes.'

I stared at the harness of my lederhosen. There were two deer and a man in a hat with a small feather embossed onto the soft leather.

'He's had a hard life . . . poor bugger. His garden means a lot.' Then she ground her teeth together and looked at me. 'Don't you *dare* wince.'

We walked down to the end. A tiny wooden jetty sloped out a few feet into a fast-flowing, icy, clear brook. Opa said that the water flowed into the River Elbe about a kilometre away, which divided East and West Germany. He plucked a peapod from its plant and broke it open before swallowing the contents in one mouthful. He put the empty pod in the brook and watched it float away round the bend. 'FOR THE RUSSIANS,' he said. 'THE SWINE.'

He turned round to face the plants, trees, flowers and vegetables, raising his arms like a priest. 'HERE IS EVERYTHING. EVERYTHING I COULD POSSIBLY NEED. POTATOES AND FRUIT AND PEAS AND BEAUTIFUL FLOWERS. I NEED NOTHING.'

I thought of our own garden back home with its carefully manicured lawns and pretty borders. Nothing like this. My father hated vegetables and would only eat frozen peas. In the distance, I could hear him trying to get the cricket score on the car radio. As we came out and Opa carefully padlocked the gate once more, my father called over: 'Warwickshire 145–3. But Barber's still in.'

Opa said, 'Six committeemen sitting round a table.' Apart from 'Good sloping' before we went to bed, they were the only English words he had ever uttered.

My father looked up. 'JA, PAPA,' he countered, absolutely exhausting his German vocabulary in one go.

My mother waved the carrots she had pulled out of the ground under his nose. 'Smashing,' she said, 'we'll have these for tea.'

Every morning that my father was in Germany, he would drive to Luneburg, almost forty miles away, to buy an English newspaper that would be only two days out of date.

My mother would come downstairs into the kitchen, look at the clock, tap it and say, 'The old man's been fiddling with it again.' Then she'd put it forward by a quarter of an hour, pick up the small tin urn that always stood next to the sink and ask me to come into the village with her.

Opa would be outside in the yard, feeding the pigs, chopping wood or tending the vegetables. He would move on to these practical tasks only after he'd replaced the three gnomes and the red windmill in the front garden. He took them in every night to stop them being stolen. 'Round here, garden ornaments matter,' my mother explained. 'Look at next door. They've only got a Bambi, and that's lost a leg.'

We walked on up a quiet road lined by new houses built by their owners. The ground between them was packed with small allotments, all containing their own neat rows of vegetables. Old women, mostly dressed in black, were bent crooked over the earth, every day of the summer.

A small bar where men got drunk on Sundays lay at the foot of a steep, straight hill. At the top of the hill lay the village cemetery. 'Oma and Uncle Wilhelm are up there,' said my mother. 'We must take them some flowers and give them a good raking before the end of the week.'

When we reached the village's main road, we turned right, past the Aral garage and the blacksmith's – both run by Heinz, who used to pull my mother's pigtails and carry her bag when she was a schoolgirl. We stopped at a large white house. The paint on the front was still pock-marked with bullet holes left over from the fighting twenty years ago. A small white gate had a sign on it; 'ACHTUNG, STUFE!' For several years I had thought of this as a relic from the war, warning of the approach of an enemy plane. In fact, it said, 'BEWARE OF THE STEP!'

My mother went through the gate to visit her aunt, Tante Henni. She owned the house, but rented most of it out. I was sent further on up the street to get the milk from old Hinrichs.

'Here's the money for the milk. And for an ice-cream,' she instructed. 'But get the ice-cream from Klinks the butcher.'

'Why?' I asked.

'Because Hinrichs is a mean little man. Always has been. We don't want to give him any more money than we can help. Just the milk. And some ointment for your father's ears. They're waxing up again.'

After Herr Hinrich has siphoned two litres of milk into the tin churn, I thanked him. 'PLEASE,' he said. 'AND AN ICE-CREAM?'

'NO, THANK YOU. MY MOTHER DOESN'T BELIEVE IN SWEET THINGS,' I lied.

'HOW ENGLAND'S CHANGED HER,' he sighed, and turned to straighten the salamis hanging from the shelf behind him.

After I'd bought the ice-cream from Klinks', I went into Tante Henni's back garden, picked a carrot and washed it in the brook before eating it. As I walked up the path towards the house, I saw Heinella, the man who lived downstairs, cutting the head off a goose. He was humming a waltz. There was a pile of seven other beaked faces at his feet, attached to plump bodies and floppy necks, which lay at unnatural angles.

Heinella was about forty and strongly built. When he was young, he'd been a fine carpenter, but an accident had damaged the nerves in one of his hands.

Now the years were gone, and he was a builder. He liked to speak English to me.

'For you,' he said, holding up a goose and smiling whilst the blood poured out over his forearms.

'NO, THANK YOU.'

'IN ENGLISH,' he said, in German.

'No, thank you.'

He laughed and threw a broken beak on to the compost heap.

Such good news about Papa. Being able to work will make things easier, although the old goat will also find drinking partners again. Watch him. He sicks like a hose. Don't stand any nonsense.

And don't try to blind me with your cats and foul gases. Even if what's-his-name Schrödinger did 'prove' that a cat couldn't be both alive and dead at the same time, why shouldn't reality be ludicrous? Or senseless? Or just plain stupid?

My news is not startling: Mrs Bacon's wedding and engagement rings (not big rocks, but nice enough) no longer fit over her swollen knuckles. They cause her pain. She never complains directly to the Reverend though, and was reluctant to take them off altogether. I suppose she believes in something – and anyway, he would 'tsk' about it. It was me who eventually informed old Bacon about the rings, and he must have told Peter Slythe; a jeweller came to the vicarage only yesterday.

He is tall, dark, mid-thirties, well-built but lean enough. His face is 'sculpted' and stuck in the middle of it is a long, sharp and exceedingly large nose, thin lips, and uncertain smile and brown eyes which never look at anything directly. His manner is courteous, shy but with willing good humour, and his voice is deep and soft at the same time, a bear whispering. He smells slightly of oil and is dressed in a smart, fashionable manner – that is, discreet tweed jacket, double-breasted with broad shoulders, tapering to his hips with wide, turned-up trousers; but no hat, no thin mous-tache, no pipe.

What are you going to do about that, Rainer? I do like the shy ones, and he has an eye for me. A few soft words wouldn't harm you. Try some.

He helped to ease Mrs Bacon's rings off her finger – I gave him some lard – and took some measurements, and said that he would be back with the different sizings in only a few days.

I'm glad that Captain Fitzgerald has gone back to America. He'll be fine – Americans always are; they aren't allowed to be disappointed for too long – and anyway, from what the newspapers here are saying, there aren't many shortages there. No – my heart does definitely not go out to Captain Fitzgerald. Everyone here moans that the Americans seem to be sending all kinds of aid to you, Rainer, whilst 'poor old England' starves. Well, the Bacons are doing very nicely, thank you, and I'm sending you yet more tins of tongue.

You're starving me, Rainer. I'm glad that the hat is too

small. Maybe it wouldn't be if you thought less of your head.

Nr. Stratford. November 23rd, 1947

My mother's cooking improved when we went to Germany. She took pleasure in tugging the carrots out of the rich earth and scooping potatoes up, getting the thick brown soil wedged underneath her fingernails.

She spent hours preparing meals, time that she would never have given up in England. Meatballs were created by moulding minced meat, flour, onions and spices together. Jams were made in cavernous metal cookpots which were carefully boiled on the old stove, heated by the logs Opa had recently chopped. Anything that was not eaten was preserved in sealed jars and stored in the cool cellars. Opa could eat from these in the winter, and my mother took anything he didn't want back home in the Mini. Every space in the small car was filled with jars of gherkins, asparagus, jam, peas, beans and strawberries.

We went on mushroom hunts, collecting large yellow fungii in battered canvas bags for my mother to cook in what she called a 'fry up'. Our favourite hunt took us across several fields and into a wood which was cool and moist, untouched by the sun even during the hottest summers.

One side of the wood ended on a steep sandy slope which overlooked the River Elbe. We slithered down it to the café at the bottom. There, she bought me a Coke and gave me twenty-five pfennigs for the jukebox. I always played 'If you're going to San Francisco, be sure to wear some flowers in your hair'.

Often, there would be an American patrol at the café, relaxing after a spell of duty looking across the river at the Russians in their watchtowers. My mother would put her lipstick on and have a coffee with a captain or lieutenant, even a sergeant. Once, I got a ride in a jeep from a man called Kowalski.

'That doesn't sound very American to me,' I said.

He gave me some gum. 'That's the beauty of it, fella,' Kowalski replied, 'nobody in the States really comes from the place.'

'I see,' I said, without seeing at all.

My mother said she liked the Americans. They gave her a feeling of well-being and reminded her of the time at the end of the war when they'd helped her.

'In what way?' I asked.

She pulled up her sleeve and brandished the orange segment schrapnel wound. 'With this. They drove me to the hospital every day for two weeks to get it dressed and bandaged.'

'Why?'

'Because it was infected, and weeping badly.'

'Who took you?'

'The Americans.'

'Which Americans?'

'Just some Americans.'

This didn't seem like a satisfactory reply, but it had to do. It didn't seem right to disturb her. She liked her life in Germany, with its memories, simple rhythms and wholesome activities. Nobody fussed when she did the housework and took off her clothes or caught flies and fed them to the spiders in the garden. The village had either seen it all before or had more important things to worry about.

Her soul had escaped from the effects of Time, and Time must have dropped away from her, too.

The next morning, Opa took me to Luneburg for an ice-cream. He did this once every week, whilst my mother went to visit old friends in the neighbouring villages and my father drove around trying to find high ground for improved radio reception. This time, we left later than planned.

The previous night, 'Deutschland' had triumphed over England in the television game of *It's a Knockout!* England had been represented by Tewkesbury, but this didn't matter to Opa. He sang 'Deutschland Über Alles', stood rigidly to attention and drank too much beer. Afterwards, he'd fallen asleep on the sofa and urinated all over the tartan rug that covered it. My mother simply pulled his trousers off and dragged him feet first to his bedroom. She started to ask my father to help, but then thought better of it, and did the job herself.

'Let him stew in his piss,' she said, before disappearing downstairs to put the trousers and the rug into the stone washing tub, which still had to be heated by lighting a fire beneath it.

The drive to Luneburg in Opa's grey Volkswagen Beetle was quiet, disturbed only by his persistent sniffing and the odd comment about the fertile landscape. Once he asked how Nanna was – 'THE OLD WITCH' he called her – and when I said that she was very well, he said, 'SKINNY BIRDS LIKE THAT LIVE FOR AGES. SHE LOOKS AFTER HERSELF THAT ONE, BUT SHE'S CRUEL TO YOUR MOTHER. MAKE SURE YOU LOOK AFTER HER WHEN SHE'S OLD. DON'T LET HER BECOME LONELY.'

All this was said without a trace of emotion disturbing his square-set, neat yet determined features. I thought of Oma, and Elspeth, who had just left him because he was always rude to her. She was a good twenty stones, and Opa used to puff his cheeks out and laugh whenever she beat him at cards or hid his beer. Before that, Martha had helped to look after him, but his drinking had eventually seen her off, too. Even Peter the cat had run away, or maybe drowned in the brook chasing rats.

He changed the subject and roared with delight as his little car gradually accelerated to one hundred kilometres an hour, telling me with sharp certainty that, 'THE VOLKSWAGEN IS THE FINEST CAR IN THE WORLD!'

He became quieter as we crossed Luneburg Heath, where the German surrender had been received at the end of the war, and then more cheerful again as we entered the old town itself.

Luneburg seemed to belong to a different age. It didn't have shopping precincts and new health centres, or even pock-marked walls. Bach had once played on the cathedral organ and heavy weeping willows poured themselves on to the road that crossed the bridge into the main square. The streets were cobbled, and the ornate Town Hall was called the 'Rathaus'. It had a clocktower coloured dark green and gold. Every hour a procession of wooden figures emerged from a secret place to hit the bells lined up conveniently in front of them.

Before buying the ice-cream, I went to the public toilets in the square. A matronly figure dressed in white overalls sat at the entrance to the men's side, a saucerful of ten-pfennig pieces on the small table in front of her. I entered the nearest cubicle, and had only just got in when the woman unlocked the door and asked me if everything was all right.

'YES, THANK YOU,' I said.

'I COULD MOP THE FLOOR IF YOU LIKE,' she persisted. 'OR PUT SOME DISINFECTANT INTO THE BOWL TO MAKE IT ESPECIALLY CLEAN . . .'

I felt the first flush of embarrassment, and struggled with the complex arrangement of zips and harness on my lederhosen before saying I'd finished anyway, and left to find Opa.

He was sitting on a bench, barking into cupped hands and laughing as people looked round, startled, expecting to see a small dog. It felt like Tatters at the football again, and I was thankful that Opa hadn't brought his 'Laughsac' with him. The last time we'd come to Luneburg, he'd placed it under a chair in a café and then sat back to enjoy the puzzled, slightly alarmed expressions on people's faces as they heard the prerecorded, chattering cackles that cut the air somewhere beneath them.

The Italian ice-cream shop was just across the road. Italian ices were considered very exotic, and I had banana, chocolate, vanilla, raspberry and mint, whilst Opa had a scoop of blueberry with a squirt of cream, which seemed very sophisticated. We went to the delicatessen to buy my mother a jellied fish, found a newpaper with some cricket scores in it for my father, and went home.

On the way back, Opa told me about his neighbours. He was convinced that for some time they'd been looking over their fence and into his backyard, spying on him. He even thought they coveted the little red windmill, and described the envy on their faces whenever there was a good wind. I tried to smile, and Opa gestured to his purse on the back seat.

'TAKE 150 MARKS,' he said. 'BUT DON'T TELL YOUR MOTHER. SHE WOULDN'T APPROVE.'

I'd been taught to look surprised and reluctant at moments like this. I opened my mouth slightly and became diffident; but Opa insisted. 'I HAVE A GOOD PENSION. I WANT FOR NOTHING. I HAVE WORKED HARD ALL MY LIFE. THERE IS PLENTY OF MONEY. TAKE IT. I ONLY SEE YOU ONCE A YEAR. GO ON – OR I'LL ONLY SPENT IT ON BOOZE.'

With a look of grateful humility, I took the money.

As we neared home, Opa cut the engine and the car coasted the last 400 yards in silence along the quiet road, past the bar where men were already singing loudly, and past the allotments where the women were still coaxing their vegetables. We turned through the gate at the top of the drive, and freewheeled down the steep incline into the backyard, stopping just before the grey garage doors. Opa adjusted his rear-view mirror. 'THEY'RE CHECKING ON ME,' he said. 'DON'T LOOK! THEY'LL THINK I'VE NOTICED. OPEN THE DOOR SLOWLY AND CLOSE THE GATE.'

Whilst I was doing this, he pushed the car a few yards forward, so that it rested underneath the apple tree that always gave sour apples but plenty of shade. From this new angle, and with the dark branches obscuring their view, the neighbours would not be able to see Opa. He flipped open the Volkswagen's boot, and set about the engine with a white rag and a pot of yellow grease.

His muscular arm bulged and rippled as he vigorously rubbed the metal, and after only a few minutes it was a gleaming silver colour. Next, he fetched a bucket of water from the brook and washed the tyres down. Finally, he took another piece of cloth and flicked any traces of dirt or dust from the car's shell. It was a routine he maintained every time he went for a drive. I didn't mind because he'd promised to leave it to me in his will.

After parking the old but still pristine vehicle back in the garage, he raised himself up on to the iron frame which was once a swing but was now used for beating carpets and Opa's exercises. He completed twenty-five chin-ups, his tight body in full control as he brought his chin exactly level with the bar every time. He jumped down, flexed an impressive arm in my direction, glanced fondly at his Beetle and threw a contemptuous glance at his neighbour's house.

'GOOD, YES?' he said. 'I HAVE STRENGTH. AND BRAINS.'

The next morning, I woke up to the sound of a shovel scraping urgently against the ground. It hesitated for a few seconds, and then started again. This pattern repeated itself many times before I became curious enough to get out of bed and wander downstairs.

In the backyard, a brick wall about twelve feet high had already been built. Two supporting green rods stuck out of it at an angle of forty-five degrees, like stanchions attached to goal posts. The bottom three feet had already been sealed with a rough, stippled covering of cement. Opa was mixing the next batch now. The noise I had heard was him scooping the cement up before turning it over.

'THEY'LL NEVER SEE ME NOW,' he smirked, sticking his tongue out towards the nosy neighbours, and asserting his new-found privacy. He sniffed loudly, told me about his muscles again and said that the German army was still the best in the world.

My mother was sitting in her swimsuit shelling peas at the small garden table. 'He's talking shit,' she said, without looking up. 'They even issue them with hairnets now. Hippies – that's all they are. HAIR-NETS,' she shouted provocatively at Opa, who waved a dismissive arm at her and continued to mix his cement.

'Have you seen the Berlin Wall?'

I nodded.

'I hope the anti-social old bugger drives into it one night. Go and get him some beer. And if you see your father, tell him I need taking to T.H.'s this afternoon.' When we were talking in English, my mother now referred to Tante Henni as 'T.H.', because Opa was increasingly jealous of her. They'd even stopped playing cards.

On the way to get the beer, I met the post-lady on her yellow bike.

'POST, PLEASE,' I piped.

She delved into the yawning black leather bag on the front of the bike. 'ONE FOR YOU, SOMETHING FOR YOUR GRANDFATHER AND A LETTER FROM YOUR MOTHER'S FRIEND IN HAMBURG – THE ONE WHO GOES TO HEALTH FARMS. NOTHING FOR YOUR FATHER.'

This was often the best moment of the day. Last week, I'd had a letter from Mark Perkins telling me about his holiday in Wales. I was good at letters, and had already written to him several times. My mother had remarked that neither 'that Murray or the boy with the plate in his head had written'. She still approved of Mark. Aunty Betty had written about the fortnight she'd spent on her cousins' farm in Cornwall. They were a bad lot, and Aunty Betty had been trying to save them. 'My dear,' she wrote, 'I was reading Kings, chapter 22, verse 17 – and there it was! "I saw all Israel scattered upon the hills, as sheep that did not have a shepherd." Well – if that wasn't an invitation! Thanks be that I'd brought my tape recorder and kept a packet of bourbons back; at least the children will be saved . . .'

This time I had three neatly rolled comics from Nanna and Tatters – the *Valiant*, the *Victor* and *Look and Learn*. There was always a short note with them. This one read, 'Life is quiet. The new football season starts soon – mind you, that's nothing to look forward to with the lot they've got at the moment. Hope the comics are what you want. Love N and T.'

I bought the beer from the family across the road, who kept a large supply cooling in their cellars. The post in my hand reminded me of the letters I'd seen packed in Tatters' safe back in England. I wanted to see them. Letters now seemed magical, and contained important, secret information, especially those that had been kept rather than thrown away.

Usually people wanted to forget the past because it was messy or awkward. That's why they destroyed things, or lost them. They don't mind memory because it's unreliable; and besides, it's easy to change the facts. Opa kept his car and his muscles. That's what he wanted to remember. They provided an unbroken continuity with the past, neatly preserving its most admirable parts.

But letters are different. They can only bring the past into the present for a quick moment before becoming history. They can't preserve anything.

'Life is quiet.' Life had been quiet when Tatters wrote that. It could still be quiet. But looking at the letter when it wasn't quiet wouldn't help. It wouldn't convince anybody; not like Opa's muscles. You

couldn't deny those, or take them away from him.
Not yet, anyway. He wasn't ready.

Pehaps the letters held some unassailable truth
which Tatters wanted to believe. But no more than
that – they had no effect on the present. Aunty Betty
had once read to me from Corinthians: 'the letter
killeth, but the spirit giveth life'.

When I got back with the beer, Opa and my mother
were playing cards. She took a puff of her cigarette
and spoke casually to me in English. 'Has he got the
K. of H.?' I saw the King of Hearts and nodded.
Without quite knowing why, Opa pulled his cards
into his chest so that I couldn't see them any more. It
had always been this way when they played cards
together.

*You ask for signs of the affection which you must already
know I hold for you. What further proof do you require?
My staying with your Mama and Papa whilst you are in
England, my help in building your home, my tolerance of
Captain Fitzgerald? The letters I continue to write? Do I
really have anything else to prove?*

*Should I compete with the exquisite descriptions of love
in (let's say) Goethe or Flaubert? Should I draw phrases
from them before substituting your name and circumstances
at the appropriate moments and claim them as my own?
Does my behaviour not tell you everything you need or
should ever want to know? Maybe I could woo you in terms
of my own making – something to do with space and time?
Could we not say that we are like the particles I have*

mentioned to you, which, having arbitrarily thumped into each other once or twice (or however many times you wish), are in some way forever connected and so will instinctively 'know' the pattern, the process by which they will meet again. In the meantime, we must watch and listen, and pay attention, believing that we will meet in the future, even though we don't know exactly where or when. We must not even admit to having a strategy or even of having knowledge of one, for these things would distract us from our vigil.

It is difficult to write of love. Two people meeting, face to face, on a trembling highwire. They should like to stay up there together, embracing or passing through and into each other, but reason dictates that this is impossible. Consequently, they continue their precarious balancing until courage fails them, and they both turn around and walk carefully back the way they came. How much better and more natural to simply fall, like leaves, or maybe stars, knowing that they had touched and that somehow they would be linked together again in the future. Space, time and love's shifting balance, my dear; we must respect their rules rather than trying to impose own own.

I once read about a group in Cambridge which said that biology is to do with love and physics is to do with power. I suppose that in this case, I must be more of a physicist (though I wonder how power and love are connected). I believe that I must find out more about the nature of the world, combine physics with biology, and perhaps accept that I am a part of the process that I am so keen to study and pass comment on.

Have patience.

Your father is easily up to his work. There is only a little manual labour, and he is delighted at the metal cool-box *(full of bottled water) to keep him company. One day, it will contain beer. That is something to aim for. He is also confident of obtaining well-made bricks at a discounted price.*

The winter will be hard, but we shall live in the completed cellars of the house – grey, square, cool and strong. I wonder if that is the time at which the pattern of things will draw us together again? Until then, I remain your beloved Rainer. Luneburg. December 7th, 1947.

Ten days later, my father returned to England alone to 'keep the business going'. Opa thought he worked too hard and said that the graveyard was full of indispensable people. He had an affection for my father, and when I broke the roller-blind in the bedroom, my mother quickly said, 'I'll blame your father. The old goat won't mind that.'

On the morning that he left, we all stood in the backyard packing the Minis. We were to go as far as Hamburg with him, where my mother's old school-friend Nati-Nati lived. Opa was looking up at the sky, tracing the path of an aeroplane as it followed the River Elbe, probably headed towards West Berlin.

'DEFINITELY A LUFTHANSA. THE FINEST AIRLINE.'

He asked my father why he never flew.

'I don't like flying. I need to be in control – I can't trust the pilots.'

'HE SAYS HE'S SO SCARED HE'D PEE HIS PANTS,' my mother translated, and Opa sniffed loudly.

'HE COULD STAY LONGER IF HE FLEW.'

My mother was adamant. 'IT'S EXPENSIVE. WE HAVEN'T GOT MONEY COMING OUT OF OUR EARS.'

Opa lit his pipe. 'BUT YOU'RE ALL RIGHT? I HAVE A GOOD PENSION. ALWAYS REMEMBER THAT . . .'

'KEEP YOUR MONEY, PAPA. BUY YOURSELF SOME BEER.'

My father listened to this with a mild bewilderment. He asked my mother whether she'd packed last Tuesday's *Telegraph*. She gave him a savage glance and he looked the other way, and then shook hands with Opa who embraced him and slapped him hard on the back several times. All he could manage to the energetic 'SAFE JOURNEY's and 'DRIVE CAREFULLY's was, 'JA, PAPA, JA, JA, JA, BITTE . . .'

We started for Hamburg, and my mother broke out the saltsticks. As in England, the two Minis drove in convoy, now through a series of small villages which seemed like copies of each other. Apart from the post offices and churches, most had a stork's nest, usually on top of a large barn.

My mother told me how the storks were getting ready to emigrate for the winter, and were feeding up the young, ready for the journey.

The villages seemed full of old people, all dressed in black and sitting quietly outside their houses on wooden benches. The men smoked pipes and leant forward on walking sticks, stroking grey stubble and contemplating lost dreams. The women chatted to each other in a rather dour manner, and peeled potatoes into brown enamel bowls or read catalogues from the large department stores in distant towns. Once a week, the bread and meat vans would drive into the village; people bought from them – there were no shops.

Time almost stood still in places like these. The people were getting older, but the circumstances remained constant. In one hamlet, they had built a bigger bridge over the river which ran along its boundary. One night, the old policeman was driving home, a little drunk after a night in the bar. He had forgotten about the new bridge, and took his accustomed route towards the old one, which was no longer there. His car went off the road and ploughed down the river bank. The policeman broke his neck. No more bridges were built and his car was left where it overturned. Now a family of ducks used it as shelter from bad weather.

I wondered whether the storks would ever go, but this year, like every year, they were still there. They stood on one leg, looking like weather vanes.

Almost without warning, the line of villages ended and we manoeuvred onto the busy autobahn which took us the rest of the way into Hamburg.

Our first stop was at Uncle Karl's and Tante Walda's. Uncle Karl was a retired cabinet-maker who still played the tuba for an orchestra of woodworkers. He had the beginnings of Parkinson's Disease, and in his frustration had taken to drink. My mother said that when he and Opa got together, she always had a spare pair of trousers and a plastic sheet ready, just in case.

Tante Walda was a slightly stooped, anxious little woman who walked with small jerky movements, like a bird, and never seemed to be out of an apron. Her only real loves were her budgerigars. Since I could remember, she'd had five of them. Four were lain out neatly at the bottom of the window-box on the balcony, buried under an explosion of poppies. The last one had flown away and been caught by a cat, so now she was always careful not to leave doors and windows open.

We had a frankfurter and salad for lunch, and then Uncle Karl opened a bottle of schnapps. Soon there were cups of coffee on the table, and then a selection of cream cakes arrived on gold-rimmed plates with special forks. Cigarette smoke filled the air, and there was a lot of talk about how much cleaner Germany was than England. Then my mother started to praise the Hamburg underground system, saying that she'd never take her car into the centre of town, whereas in Birmingham you didn't have much choice.

I told my father a little of what was being said.

'Birmingham's got more miles of canals than Venice,' he countered.

'HE SAYS THAT BIRMINGHAM'S BETTER THAN VENICE,' my mother said.

Everybody laughed, and Tante Walde clucked doubtfully. She went to get her budgie from the kitchen, and allowed it to hop around the table, pecking at the sugar-coated crumbs from the cakes.

'ENGLAND HAS SOME FINE COMPOSERS,'
Uncle Karl said by way of vague compromise.

'THAT ONE ONLY LISTENS TO JAZZ.'

Tante Walda had bent her head right down to the budgie's beak. 'HE CAN SAY HIS NAME – LISTEN. BUDGIE, BUDGIE, BUDGIE.' The small bird blinked at her and then hopped on to the edge of another plate. 'HE'S SUCH A CLEVER BIRD. SOMETIMES HE WHISTLES.'

Uncle Karl was leaning towards my father. 'BUT THERE ARE SOME GOOD JAZZ MUSICIANS IN ENGLAND, AREN'T THERE? CHARLIE PARKER? HE SOUNDS ENGLISH.' I could smell the sharp alcohol from the other side of the table. 'TED HEATH'S BIG BAND . . .?'

'COME ON. BUDGIE, BUDGIE, BUDGIE . . .'

My father wanted a drink of water, and started for the kitchen. As he opened the door, Budgie frantically started to flap his wings, and with a great effort lifted himself clear of the table and headed for the open air. There was a sound like washing drying in the wind.

'SHUT THE DOOR!' squawked Tante Walda.

My father moved his head slowly from side to side, like a tortoise, although his eyes were full of panic.

'The door. Shut it. *Quickly*,' snapped my mother.

He jumped back into the room and pulled the door towards him. Budgie was cut neatly in two. The back half dropped at my father's feet, and when he opened the door again, we saw that the head and neck had fallen on to the telephone desk in the hall. My mother quickly gathered the bits up and wrapped them in my copy of the *Victor*. Tante Walda was croaking with grief, large tears rolling unchecked down her face. Uncle Karl announced that he would play a requiem for Budgie on his tuba and, on his way out, fell onto my chair and pressed a five-mark coin into my hand. 'BEST GET SOME MORE POPPIES,' he said. 'THE PURPLES LOOK GOOD AT THE MOMENT.'

We were staying overnight at Krista and Rolf Munsterman's house, about fifteen minutes' drive from Tante Walda and Uncle Karl, whom we left in a mood of bewildered mourning. The Munstermans were Nati-Nati's friends, and my mother was put out that we weren't staying with her, and talked every minute of the short journey. 'She's getting fatter and fatter. She's worse every year, you know. One of these days, she'll explode. I bet you've never seen her cook. She's that lazy. Bone idle. Never lifts a finger, that one. Never. Not in all the time I've known her, which is longer than I care to remember, I can tell you . . .'

I liked staying at Tante Krista and Uncle Rolf's. He was a farmer, and obviously very wealthy. 'They sometimes do the roulette wheel,' my mother warned, making it sound like a particularly attractive sin.

The bedrooms were vast, and each one contained a sink with a mixer tap arrangement that you would usually only see in the better hotels. My father and I were allowed to take bottles of Coca-Cola from the fridge whenever we wanted. The wall which trailed the semicircular staircase was studded with mounted deer heads, shot in the grounds. The Munstermans had two Mercedes and one BMW; they even had separate bedrooms.

When they greeted us, Tante Krista said it was a pity that my father was only staying for one night. Uncle Rolf told him not to worry, and that his family would be in good hands after he'd gone. My father nodded rather tamely as my mother gave him her usual approximate translation. Then Tante Krista scowled at Uncle Rolf and told him to go and take one of his pills as he appeared to be getting too red in the face.

That evening, whilst the Munstermans were out at their club, we went to the Dome, a fair in the St Pauli district of the city. We didn't attempt any of the rides due to my father's indigestion. 'Applecake always does this to him,' my mother said rather sourly, 'he really ought to learn to eat within his limitations.'

We only managed the Hall of Mirrors, where we all stood facing our distorted reflections in the first chamber. My mother's head was elongated so that it became twice the length of her body, my father shrunk to the size of a toadstool and I became taller than both of them, though no fatter than a pipe-cleaner.

'It's all fuzz and muzz,' my mother said. She hated anything indistinct or uncertain.

Her wrinkles were exaggerated so that her face looked like a ploughed field, whilst my father's tight-lipped grimace became his most prominent feature, spread between two elastic, puffy cheeks. 'Sourpuss,' my mother sneered. And then, 'I must get some more of that cream. But I'm afraid there's no helping you.'

She looked pityingly at him as he stared despairingly at the stubby frailty of the image before him. I wondered what it would be like when they were both old and stooped, but my mother stopped any nonsense by taking her front teeth out and pulling a grotesque face into the mirror.

We had sausage and lemonade at a small café outside the Dome. I asked my father why we didn't have as much money as Tante Krista and Uncle Rolf. He said it was to do with 'opportunity' and taking it quickly when it came along. He told me to keep a sharp lookout for it, as he rather thought it had been and gone without him quite noticing it. Then he spilt his drink down his trousers, and said that, as time went on, it became more difficult to distinguish it. With an efficient flourish, my mother took a scented wipe from her handbag and vigorously rubbed the soiled leg. She said that Chance had nothing to do with it, and that Nanna had spent all the money and that I wasn't to forget to notice the size of her diamond cluster the next time I saw her.

A waitress in a short skirt walked over and made a great fuss about my father's trousers before she suddenly sat down in his lap. She asked him if he wanted anything else. He started to move his hand from left to right in quick, nervous jerks, speaking to her in broken English; 'No . . . my leg . . . the drink . . . cloth . . . everything OK. Thank you.'

My mother was laughing uncontrollably, her head bent backwards, the tears rolling down her face like small pebbles. 'Oh dear . . . oh dear . . .' The waitress' hand was now on the damp patch, and massaging it slowly with careful sweeping movements.

My father was losing his temper. 'Can't you help? Tell her to go away. Something, at least.'

Between little snorts of pleasure, my mother said, 'It's not a she. It's a he. A man. Oh dear . . . we're in one of those funny clubs.'

The man in the short skirt understood what she was saying and climbed off my father's knee. He left a large oval kiss on his cheek and headed back inside to the bar, tottering slightly on high heels. Again, my mother reached down and brought out a scented wipe.

The next day, we waved my father off on his way to the Hook of Holland. My mother had made him a large pack of gherkin and salami sandwiches trapped between slices of dark brown ryebread. Out of habit, he eyed them suspiciously.

'You're a fussy bugger,' she said. 'I've taken the rind off.'

'Any cake?'

'No fear. You get your own cake. I'm not made of money. A bar of chocolate. And don't forget to send me two hundred pounds. I'll go to the bank in Luneburg to get it. You haven't lost the address?'

My father patted his back pocket, where he kept his wallet.

'Don't drive too fast. Not in that small car. You know what they're like on the autobahn.'

They bent forwards, moving like two cranes on a

building site, their lips brushing each other's cheeks before they straightened up again.

After he'd gone, my mother said, 'I bet he's forgotten something. Never mind . . . poor old devil. There'll be a hell of a mess for me to clear up when we get home. Four weeks. What'll he do with himself? I dread to think. Come on; we're going to the shops.'

We travelled into the centre of Hamburg by underground. Outside the station was a life-size bronze sculpture of a naked man. As we walked past, she said, 'He's got nothing to write home about. Either that or those vandals have been at him again.'

On the train, she told me Opa had been a policeman in Hamburg before the war, had been able to run ten kilometres in under thirty minutes and had been the North German middleweight boxing champion.

The middle of the city was entirely modern, except for the cathedral-like railway station, a vast semicircular dome of glass and weathered metal, which the British had tried to bomb many times, and failed. 'Mind you, they flattened everything else,' she said confidentially. 'The bombers used the Alster Lake to tell them where Hamburg was. We used to camouflage it so they couldn't see where we were.'

'How?' I asked.

'Tarpaulins, pulled right across.'

I looked puzzled. Surely nobody would be fooled by this.

'So they couldn't see the water moving. Of course, if was useless during the day bombing, later on. Bloody stupid, in fact. I had a friend who was hit by a fire bomb after lunch on a Tuesday. Her whole body

125

was alight. She couldn't put the flames out, and had to slide underneath the edge of the tarpaulin to get to the water.'

'What happened? Did she burn to death?'

'No. She drowned.'

We walked into the handbag shop. My mother was set on a crocodile one, like Tante Krista had. 'Not as expensive, but nice enough.'

She did several circuits around the shop, each time with a different pattern of crocodile on her arm, stopping casually at the mirror and taking in the general effect.

Then we went to the art gallery to meet Nati-Nati for lunch. 'She's not at all interested in art,' my mother said, 'but it makes her happy.'

We arrived early, and looked at the pictures before going through to the restaurant. She walked at a brisk pace through the galleries, admiring the landscapes and criticising everything else. 'That's smashing,' she said, or 'I wouldn't mind that,' and, 'At least you can see what it's meant to be.'

I found a painting by someone called Claude, who sounded very English. A label to the right said, 'Aeneas's Farewell in Carthage. 1676'. A woman was pointing to boats in a harbour. She was looking directly at a man, and they both seemed very preoccupied. On the horizon was a bright light, warm and pinkish, but there was a dark cloud right over the two figures at the front of the painting. Everyone was acting in a polite, official way. I wondered whether the man and woman were in love. I thought they were, but it was difficult to tell. I thought of my parents parting a few hours earlier; were they in love?

My mother stood behind me. 'Nice dogs. He could do dogs all right. Come on. There's a Van Gogh in the next room.' She pronounced it like a caricatured Scotsman, 'Van G-Och.' 'He cut his ears off, you know.'

We met Nati-Nati in the restaurant a few minutes later. She had already squeezed herself into a small plastic chair. There was a smell of cologne and her face had a glossy, damp transparency. Her husband was a chemist, and she'd brought me some wart cream.

'THANK YOU,' I said, and bent my knees to kiss her.

She ordered a small carrot and sultana salad, and then had a cream cake and coffee for dessert.

'THAT WON'T DO YOU MUCH GOOD, NATI,' my mother said.

'AT THE HEALTH FARM THEY SAID I NEEDED TO KEEP MY SUGAR LEVEL UP. I DO HAVE AN EXCEPTIONALLY HIGH METABOLISM.'

They talked about her most recent visit to the farm, how much it cost, and Nati-Nati's sister, Mellie, who was a dentist in Hanover. They remembered school, friends they hadn't seen for a long time, and those who'd died in the war. Although it was twenty years ago, they still shed tears and worried about the cost of funerals. 'We were better off then,' my mother said. 'Just throwing you on a pile, burning you. That's the way to go. I want to be cremated. Very clean.' Her eyes watered, and she took another mouthful of buttercake.

I had a glass of milk and my mother gave me last week's copy of the *Valiant*. Then she unwrapped a new packet of cigarettes.

'SOME OF THESE PAINTINGS ARE LOVELY. NOT ALL BY ANY MEANS – BUT CERTAINLY SOME.'

'I LIKE THE ONE WITH THE TREES.'

'BUT THEY'RE SO EXPENSIVE. I READ ABOUT ONE GOING FOR THOUSANDS ONLY LAST WEEK . . .'

'WELL, THERE'S A LOT OF MONEY IN IT THESE DAYS. MORE THAN IN THE JEWEL-LERY TRADE . . .'

'OR IN BEING A CHEMIST . . .'

'WE SHOULD HAVE MARRIED ARTISTS.'

The two women laughed. There were lipstick marks all round the rims of their coffee cups.

My mother insisted on buying Nati-Nati another cream cake, and gave me the money to get it. They continued to smoke, and then she brought out the new handbag.

'HASN'T KRISTA GOT ONE LIKE THAT?'

'I DON'T THINK SO. I'M SURE I'D HAVE NOTICED.' Then she said that she had a friend in England who painted, though it was more of a reli-gious thing than proper painting.

'BUT SHE DID DAWLISH IN OILS ONE YEAR. THE COWS WERE TERRIFIC. VERY REAL. AND POINTING THE SAME WAY, LIKE THEY ACTUALLY DO.'

Nati-Nati said she'd call round to visit us at the Munstermans before we left, and gave my mother some expensive wrinkle lotion. 'THEY SENT US SOME EXTRA BY MISTAKE,' she explained.

It was raining outside, but they both produced telescopic umbrellas and transparent plastic bonnets from their handbags. Nati-Nati was anxious in case my mother's new one got wet.

'DON'T WORRY. I SHOULDN'T THINK IT'S LEATHER FOR A MOMENT.'

Then they went their different ways, and we walked towards the underground.

The following night, with my father back in England, my mother and I decided to stay in and watch a Jerry Lewis film on television. The Munstermans were out again, so we had the large farmhouse to ourselves. We sat on a soft, black leather sofa in front of an enormous, square screen, eating peanuts and drinking Coca-Cola.

There was a white rabbit in the film, but the main character was exasperatingly stupid. It was also dubbed, and the German actor's voice didn't quite synchronise with the image of Jerry Lewis' lips on the screen. He had too much control, whereas the pictures suggested chaos and confusion.

'I think the dubbing's ever so good,' my mother remarked. 'Unless you knew, you wouldn't realise it was a different speaker. Marvellous.'

'Is the music dubbed, too?'

She paused. 'Oh, yes. I should think so. They have to re-do it all. Right from scratch. Otherwise they wouldn't be able to get the voices in the right gaps.'

As I lay in bed that night, thinking where my father was and listening to the rain coming down steadily outside, I wondered about the woman (who was really a man) who had sat on his lap. Most of all, I could remember the look of panic on his face. Not the kind of panic you see in cartoons, with the mouth wide open, gasping for air and eyes rolling all around their sockets, but more a sort of crumpled, desperate, empty look. It was as if he'd felt guilty in some way for what happened, and that my mother had caught him out. He was frightened and helpless, and she was laughing at him. I remembered how he'd once got his testicles caught in the fly of his dinner-jacket trousers before a cricket dinner. She'd laughed then, too, even though he was crying with the pain and begging her to release the zip slowly so as to relax the pressure. What kind of relationship did they have, and had they always behaved in such a way towards each other?

My father often acted as if he was trying to get away with something. He looked shifty, while my mother constantly tried to provoke or expose him. All the books I'd read implied that parents were calm, caring people. 'Wead *Wupert*,' I'd pestered when I was very young: '"That car's for us," Daddy says, "I've hired it for the holidays."/The quaint old car looks spick and span. "It's in good order," says the man./ Next day, they plan a picnic treat, Smiles Mummy, "Yes, there's one spare seat."/So Rupert sets off at a run, To find a pal to share the fun."' Families led quiet, genial lives where nothing disturbing happened, and where behaviour was clearly and harmoniously defined. The more I thought about it, the more confusing it all became. For the first time that year, I remembered the hand behind the curtain again, motioning me towards it.

Something has happened, Rainer. I must tell you about it.

Mrs Bacon had taken the children to the market in Stratford. As it was a pleasant day, she said the three of them would have lunch on the river. I didn't want to join them – I'd been with the children all through the weekend.

As soon as they'd left the house, I went to my bedroom, closed the curtains, lay down on the bed and slept for two hours. I dreamt of the village and the Elbe; someone was floating upriver; an unknown figure. I didn't know whether or not to rescue them, and just stared across at the emptiness on the other bank. Afterwards, I went downstairs to ask the Reverend – who was fretting over his next sermon – whether I could have a bath. This is a regular courtesy.

The bathroom is a small room with green tiles and a white door, bare pipes and a great green mirror. I looked at myself in it as I undressed and thought that, considering everything, I wasn't in such bad shape.

I hung my clothes behind the door and stepped into the tub. Then I turned the taps, feeling the surge of water, still such a luxury, cold and then hot. As the bath filled and its temperature increased, I lowered myself down, and was soon lost in my thoughts. The pipes rattled, the water flooded over my face. And I lay there.

A short time later, I turned my head – and realised that somebody was standing in the room, hidden in the steam!

'Who is it?'

'You don't mind that I've come in?' replied the Reverend. 'I was – haaa! – looking for my spectacles.'

'Of course. Please look for them.'

He walked across to the washbasin, keeping his eyes resolutely on the toothbrushes propped up in the mug by the window.

I pushed myself down into the far recesses of the bath.

'Is the water hot enough?'

'Just right.'

'Only sometimes it doesn't work particularly well. And how's the soap? Do you like it?' His hair was lank and beginning to droop in the steam.

'Fine.'

'It's from France – before the wretched war, of course. I saved it, and put it out for you just now, when you came down to ask for a bath.' I shifted my position, but only caused some of the bathwater to slop over the rim of the tub. It landed with a gentle splash over his shoes. His right hand was opening and then closing into a tight fist. He said, 'Well, I'd better get back to the sermon,' and shuffled out through the clouds, closing the door quietly and without fuss behind him.

I wasn't embarrassed. I've seen it all before. But in front of greasy Bacon? You must be joking.

Mrs Bacon arrived home, her husband still stuck in his study whilst I was simply tidying the kitchen ready for tea. He has never mentioned it.

Last night, before going to bed, I found an envelope on my pillow. Inside was a five-pound note. No message. I shall use it for your presents. Keep well – I'll think of you over Christmas.

Nr. Stratford. December 14th, 1947.

The rain continued to beat down on the thatched barn roof outside, making a kind of muzzled but quick thumping noise, like the slow-motion tearing of paper. Usually there was a harsh ticking when droplets ricocheted off slate or lead. Tante Krista had told me that once a month they went into the barn loft to hunt rats. Usually, they would choose a quiet, still, warm night when the rats would be tempted out into the open. Then, the small group of farm hands who had been patiently waiting ever since the sun had started to go down, would suddenly switch on the lights and blast shotguns and air rifles at the twitching grey carpet that had cautiously been knitting together. Nothing would be there tonight; the rain made too much noise.

My door opened slowly, and a thin needle of light pierced the room. Somebody edged in, and the door shut again. In the darkness, I could see a figure make its way over to the door on the other side of the room, leading into my mother's bedroom. I closed my eyes. I could tell from the smell of cologne that it was Uncle Rolf. He tried the door, but it was locked. He tapped on it, clearly but quietly, three times. There was no reply. He repeated the knocks, slightly louder this time.

133

A hoarse whispering. 'I KNOW YOU'RE IN THERE. MAY I COME IN?'

'NO YOU MAY NOT. NOW GO BACK TO YOUR BED.'

'MY WIFE DOESN'T LOVE ME. I WANT TO BE WITH YOU.'

A cough. 'NO MORE OF THIS NONSENSE, ROLF. GO AWAY. GO ON . . .'

'YOU DON'T UNDERSTAND . . .'

'OF COURSE I BLOODY UNDERSTAND. I UNDERSTAND ONLY TOO BLOODY WELL . . .'

I held my breath. There was a short, desperate pause.

'I'VE BOUGHT YOU A BRACELET.'

'I'VE GOT A BRACELET. I'M TIRED. MY SON'S ASLEEP. YOU'LL WAKE HIM UP. GO AWAY, ROLF. IF YOU DON'T BUGGER OFF, I'LL WAKE KRISTA.'

'SHE WOULDN'T CARE.'

'OH WOULDN'T SHE. WE'LL SEE ABOUT THAT.'

I thought about the rats waiting to be blown apart.

Uncle Rolf hesitated, then trudged angrily back to the door he'd entered by. He was muttering something under his breath. The door opened and closed as quickly as it had done a few minutes earlier. I let out a gush of breath, and the light came on in my mother's room. Outside, it was still raining.

The next morning we went back to Opa's. My mother didn't mention what had happened during the night. At breakfast, Tante Krista presented Uncle Rolf with his two lightly boiled eggs and the usual handful of tablets. 'YOU LOOK VERY FLUSHED THIS MORNING,' she said. 'DID YOU HAVE YOUR MEDICINE LAST NIGHT?'

'NO,' he replied with a short grunt, 'I DIDN'T.'

The week before we left Germany was hectic. Opa was busy in the garden, 'GATHERING THE HAR- VEST' as he said, whilst my mother was in the kitchen, preserving vegetables and fruits in round glass jars and then storing them in the cellars. I had to write the labels.

'How do you spell "gherkin"?' I asked.

'I don't know – how do you spell it? Just write "pickled".'

'Is that the German for gherkin.'

'No – that's "Pfeffergurke".'

I wrote down 'pickle'. When all the labelling had been done, she stacked the jars in two piles, 'one for us, and one for the old goat. He's chopped the wood, so he'll see the winter out. Do you think we'll get this lot in the Mini?'

Time went slowly over the last few days. I played football with Jürgen, whose father ran the other large shop in the village, next to Hinrichs. 'I don't like Hinrichs,' my mother announced, 'but Jürgen's father is dirty. I wouldn't go near his jellied eels. He sweats – have you ever shaken hands with him?'

I nodded.

'Well, there you are then. And his rolls have too

many sesame seeds on. He's not beyond mixing yesterday's in with the fresh, either.'

Visits to relatives and friends in the village became a little longer and, as for our arrival eight weeks ago, the best china was brought out. Mother always took Opa's old photograph album round to Tante Henni's during the last days. It was royal blue leather, with a small embossed silver circle in the bottom right-hand corner of the cover. Inside the circle were two silver flashes of what could have been electricity, or even lightning. They made the letters 'SS'. Inside the album were a series of sepia matriarchs and men with proud walrus moustaches.

The two women turned the pages carefully, smoking cigarettes, pointing, and repeating well-rehearsed lines about each of the images. There were a few of Opa in boxing shorts and his old army uniform. One page was blank; a photograph had clearly been removed, and only the yellow matt of the old glue remained. When I asked who used to be there, my mother would answer, 'Just a friend. No longer with us.'

Tante Henni said that she'd miss us, and it was a shame that we were in England for most of the year. My mother reassured her that we'd be back again in ten months' time. She looked at the strong, bitter coffee still circling its cup after having the cream stirred in, and in a quiet, sucking voice from somewhere in her stomach said, 'Ja, Ja.' She promised us her grandfather clock when she died and wept with a quiet dignity when we left her for the last time. She told me that I was 'A GOOD YOUNG BOY', and should look after my parents; then she gave me a hundred marks. Like all the elderly women in the village, she was dressed in black, although for this visit she had adorned herself with a dark grey lace shawl, 'THE LAST THING WILLI GAVE ME BEFORE HE DIED.'

The cemetery at the top of the hill was full to the brim, and the local clergyman, Pfarrer Schulz, was proud of the fact it was being extended 'RIGHT TO THE BROW, AND WHO KNOWS, DOWN THE OTHER SIDE BEFORE TOO LONG'. He had also arranged for a local cleaning firm and a landscape gardening partnership to keep the place looking 'CLEAN AND RESPECTABLE'.

'IN EXCHANGE,' he announced, 'I WILL UNDER-TAKE TO GIVE THEIR FAMILIES FREE BURIAL SERVICES.' He looked thoughtful for a few moments, before going on. 'ALSO, A DISCOUNT ON WED-DINGS, AND I'LL PUT IN A GOOD WORD WITH THE STONEMASON WHO HAS COME UP WITH REALLY NEW PATTERNS IN THE LAST FEW MONTHS.' He assured us, however, that this was not as generous as it seemed, and to be certain that he'd done his homework; neither family was very large, and at least one parent on either side was already buried. 'THE CEMETERY WILL LOOK . . . ASTOUNDING. THE BEST IN THE REGION'. He rolled the word 'wunderbar' around his mouth like a mint, emphasising it and presenting an array of gold-capped teeth.

He apologised to my mother for giving Oma the plot nearest the gate, but space had been very tight, and at least she had the privilege of being nearest the new annexe.

He had touched a nerve. 'IT'S TOO LATE NOW,' she said darkly. 'BUT EVERYBODY COMES THROUGH THAT GATE. MY RAKING GETS SCUFFED TO NOTHING. LOOK . . .' and she pointed to the sand surrounding the grave, neat lines almost obliterated by shoe prints.

The raking was my favourite job when I helped to do the graves. It reminded me of the way that the track attendants at the speedway would draw the shale together after each race so that the track was smooth again for the next one.

I fetched and carried buckets and cans of water for my mother, who carefully washed the headstones, then weeded and replanted the plots of her own mother, Uncle Willi, a distant cousin, the husband of the old lady who lived opposite Opa but was ill with elephantiasis of the throat, and an old boyfriend who'd been killed during the war.

'If I'd married him you wouldn't have been born,' she said candidly. I let her do this one by herself, and went to pour water on the anthill that was banked up against the side of the 'Martin Luther Chapel of Rest'. There was a small plaque on the wall next to the tap I'd got the water from. It said 'PRESENTED THROUGH THE GENEROSITY OF WILHELM FLASCHE – A DISTINGUISHED AND THOUGHTFUL DENTIST'.

★

My father sent two lots of comics that week, as he'd forgotten the week before. He'd written a short letter with them: 'I didn't have time to get your comics last week. Sorry – but when I realised, it was too late for the *Valiant*, so I've got you a *Victor* instead. The weather here is very bad; the speedway at Coventry was abandoned last night (Boocock won his first two rides though!), and Warwickshire drew against Glamorgan. They really need another bowler; maybe next year. Your friend Mark Perkins telephoned to ask when you were coming home. See you soon. Love Dad.' He added three kisses and enclosed a copy of *The Sports Argus*, where I read that Birmingham were playing a friendly against an Italian team.

'No letter for me, I suppose,' said my mother grimly. 'I suppose he's busy. We ought to get him some marzipan before we go.' Then she went back to slicing and preserving the carrots.

It rained again that night, and I fell asleep almost immediately.

The roller-blind that I'd broken was flapping around its supporting tube, the way that blinds did in horror films. Lace curtains billowed back and forth through the open window. A finger appeared through them, beckoning me as it used to. I went to the window. Opa had forgotten to bring the windmill and the other figures in; they were all clustered around the rockery. I climbed through the window and lowered myself on to the soil below.

In front of me, the road to my left looped towards the village, and to the right, it stretched into the countryside. I turned right, looking for the hand that should have been attached to the finger. I'd been walking for five minutes when it appeared from behind a bush at the side of the road, and gestured down into the ditch. In the ditch was a circular concrete opening leading back underneath the surface of the road. I crawled through, but the narrow entrance gave on to a breathtaking expanse of cobbled ground which stretched as far as the eye could see in all directions. In the distance, I could see truckloads of old men and women being emptied out. A few were younger, but they were bloody and mutilated. All had numbers around their necks, and I heard a guard say (his voice drifting in the wind), 'This is your new address. Don't lose it or you'll have nowhere to go.'

Another guard came up to me and asked where my number was.

'I don't have one,' I said, comically.

He was clearly well-trained. 'You'd better come this way, then.'

He took me past the other prisoners and stopped in front of a glass door. There were no walls supporting it, no building behind it. The letters on the door said 'Post Office. Open'. I went inside. There was a woman at the counter, a number of people looking round, and a team of young men putting letters into envelopes and sealing them.

'Where am I?'

The assistant looked up. 'Where everyone is . . .

eventually. You're early, so we've got a letter ready for you. The future is ahead of you. But you must never open the envelope. Don't look. You might want to change your role; but you won't be able to. People normally only get there when they're . . .' she paused for effect '. . . when they're already here.'

'But how do I know this is the right letter? You didn't even know I was coming until now when I just walked in.'

'You don't know it's the right letter? Of course you don't. That's the point.' And she laughed . . .

'Here's your tea,' my mother said. 'Last day. Don't forget we're off to the Klinks this afternoon. The old goat's got a hangover – serves him right. Give him a game of cards, and make sure he wins.'

Outside, the sun was high and the road glistened after its night-time dousing.

Herr Klink was a burly, red-faced man who seemed to be covered in a thin layer of greasy wax. He had taken over the butcher's shop from his father, and had now built the business up so that he was thought to be the best 'Fleischer' in the district.

Whilst my mother drank schnapps with the Klinks in a room that smelled of blood, their son took me upstairs to his room. Christof was eighteen, and played me 'We all live in a yellow submarine' on his guitar, and showed me the Beatles records he had collected.

'MY DAD LIKES JAZZ, MAINLY,' I said confidentially, 'BUT HE QUITE LIKES THE BEATLES, TOO. HE'S GOT "A Taste of Honey".'

'AND THE ROLLING STONES? I am also liking them.'

'No, no.' I waggled my head decisively. 'NOT EVEN ON TELEVISION.' Then I told him about the hundred pounds my mother would give me if I didn't smoke until I was twenty-one.

'I SMOKE,' he said. I'd guessed as much, and he lit a cigarette and puffed on it with extravagant intensity.

He showed me the cover of the *Abbey Road* album. 'PEOPLE SAY THAT JOHN LENNON IS DEAD BECAUSE HE ISN'T WEARING ANY SHOES.' I thought this was plain silly, though I actually nodded my head in avid agreement. We listened to 'Lucy In The Sky With Diamonds', and Christof told me it was about 'A KIND OF DREAM'. I looked confused and told him about the dream I'd had the previous night. All he could say was, 'YOU CAN'T TRUST THE POST ANY MORE.'

We went downstairs to swim in his parents' pool; everybody else was already in their costumes. Herr Klink had a large bowl of a stomach, but it was firm rather than flabby. In contrast to his red face, neck and hands, the rest of his body was vanilla white. 'NOW TO LOSE SOME OF THIS,' he roared, slapping the stomach energetically.

'What's happening over there?' I asked my mother, pointing to a large, dilapidated building behind the shop. A truck had reversed up to the entrance, and the sound of agitated knocking came violently across the yard.

'It's a "Schlachthaus".'

I didn't know the word.

She whispered. 'A slaughterhouse. They're killing some pigs.' And seeing my look of confused horror. 'You don't mind when you're eating pork, do you?'

'How do they do it?'

But by this time, there was some wild, random squealing, and the agitated click of trotters had grown to a drumming crescendo.

'They know now. They can smell it.'

'How do they do it, though?' I persisted.

'I don't know. Electrocute them. A metal bolt through the brain. How should I know? Now be quiet and let's go for a swim.'

'Does it hurt?'

'I've never tried it. I don't think so. All over in a second. And don't stare.'

Suddenly, a large pig broke through the short wooden runway that connected the back of the truck to the 'Schlachthaus' entrance. Its head was rolling loosely. It careered straight past us and plunged into the pool. There was a terrible screaming as it thrashed about hopelessly, then the water stained darkly with urine and excrement as the pig lost control of its functions. A man in a blood-stained white overall ran up to Herr Klink.

'SORRY, HERR KLINK. HE WAS TOO BIG FOR THE RUN . . .'

The butcher was trembling. 'SHOOT IT AND DRAIN THE POOL.'

Then he turned to the rest of us and said with reassuring, sweaty good humour, 'MAYBE SOME

143

LEMONADE AND CAKE. THE POOL IS TEM-
PORARILY OUT OF ACTION.'

There were no nuns aboard the *Doric Ferry* on the way
home to England, and the sea was much calmer. The
water seemed warm and sucking as we looked down
at it from the deck-rail. Slop, slop, slop, slop. The
swallowing ocean.

'Back to grubby old England,' my mother
announced.

It had never struck me as being particularly dirty.

'They know about cleanliness in Germany. Look at
the cemetery. In England, you're forgotten as soon as
you're in the ground. Nobody works on the graves.
Once a year, perhaps – but that's it.'

Slop, slop, slop, slop.

'Remind me to give Aunty Betty a pair of those
washing-up gloves. You can't get them in Birmingham. I bought five lots. They'll keep me going for
another year.'

– 5 –

A most provoking letter. Problems of Time and Space, as usual. The Reverend Bacon clearly feels that he is running out of Time and is simply inhabiting erotic Space each Time an opportunity presents itself. Doubtless, any subsequent actions would have been justified along the lines of 'true to Mrs Bacon in Time even if unfaithful in Space'. Almost 'automatic' behaviour, in fact. I must brush up on my Freud. I usually have accurate hunches about this sort of thing.

People are curious. Hinrichs' wife has just left him; I can't blame her after the way he'd been carrying on with Frau Holzenbein, but still, the circumstances were rather strange. She had been strong and discreet during the affair. But as soon as it came to an end, she disappeared and simply sent Hinrichs a note asking him to send her things on to Hanover where she'd taken up with an old boyfriend. I have no idea what sort of fellow he is.

There are many strange things like that going on here; all kinds of odd cults and societies. It sounds the same in England. I remember your experiences with Mrs Slythe's fortune-telling. But then, what can we believe in, after all? Few take the sciences seriously.

Strindberg said that even the worst marriage was better than no marriage at all? I wonder. Anyway, that's not much help with the Reverend Bacon's auto-erotic habits. I look forward to receiving the presents. In the meantime, I am impatiently your beloved Rainer.

Luneburg. December 20th, 1947.

'Hello,' I shouted, wiping my feet on the mat and then being careful to check for dirty fingerprints on the door. The house was quite still. My mother had been there when I'd left to see Mark Perkins two hours ago, and said we'd be having pickled gherkins and frank-furters for tea when I got back. A half-drunk mug of sherry stood on the draining board, and her apron had been slung almost casually over the back of a kitchen chair. There was a note on the cupboard: 'Gone to Nanna's. Come round when you get back. Love Mum.' My mother never went there unless it was Christmas, and now it was only September.

I rode there as quickly as I could, taking the short cut round the back of the golf course and trying, like speedway riders, to take the corners without using my brakes.

When I arrived, I saw that my father was also there. He was in the living room, with Nanna and my mother.

'What's happening?' I demanded.

They glanced at me, but carried on their discussion in low, hesitant voices.

'Tatters is in hospital,' someone eventually said.

My mother had made Nanna a cup of tea, and my father was left standing uncertainly between them, examining the creamy swirls in the carpet, hands behind his back, lips thin and absolutely horizontal, like a pencil line.

'Something in his blood . . .' from my mother.

'He was all right last night. He had his biscuit just before going to bed. As usual.'

'And he was at the cricket last week when Edrich made all those runs,' my father offered, in an official kind of way. He went to sit down.

'Mind the toffees,' Nanna warned. Her eyes were red and tears had ploughed small furrows in the pale foundation that caked her face.

'There, there,' my mother said, as if she was talking to Aunty Betty. She looked at my father. 'That bloody doctor. Refusing to come out last night. It's disgraceful. I bet we could have him struck off. I bet we ruddy well could . . .'

But nobody was really listening, and we sat in silence, picking our way through the shortbread until Mother decided to give the upstairs a Hoover, as she didn't think Nanna wanted to be fussed with it at a time like this.

I saw Tatters at the hospital the following day. He was yellow and looked shrivelled beneath his thin, papery-white gown.

'This is the room they put them in when they're going to die,' my mother said rather too frankly. 'I asked a nurse. Of course, he's pulled all his tubes out. Difficult old sod, but bless him.'

Almost before I knew it, everyone was back at our house after the funeral.

Uncle Peter's eyebrows moved like agitated caterpillars as he recounted the moment when Tatters' coffin wouldn't slide smoothly into its final resting place. 'Typically awkward to the end, eh.'

Earlier, there had been a problem with the traffic, and we'd arrived late. 'Posh car,' my mother said, 'don't get your hands all over the upholstery.'

The vicar reminded us that he had a wedding to dash off to, so if we could pay our last respects as quickly as possible, he'd be most grateful. There was another burial immediately afterwards, and he introduced a note of anxious levity: 'I believe the other hearse will have to make a couple of circuits while we finish in here. I assure you that there's no problem, but if we could just move things along a little. It wouldn't do to have too many . . . lain out, as it were, at the same time.'

Uncle Lance said, just loud enough, 'Don't want them lined up like fish, do we?'

'Have you no shame,' hushed Aunty Kath.

'No. Have you?' Uncle Lance had already been to the pub. Everybody gave them a 'shooshing' look.

My mother did the catering for what she proudly called 'the wake'. Aunty Betty did some sausage rolls, and there was potato salad and quiche for the main course. For starters, she'd gone exotic and cut some avocados in half and dolloped some mayonnaise into

148

the pear-shaped craters. 'You need something a little bit, well, fancy, don't you,' she said.

There were gay flowers all round the room. 'Don't throw them away. I'll put some on the grave, take some to the office and if there's any left over, Aunty Pam could do with some. Her waterworks have gone again.'

Although my father thought vanilla would be more dignified for the occasion, rum and raisin had carried the day, but it was a close run thing with the raspberry ripple. I scooped out the ice cream for everybody, and handed the bowls around.

'I can't eat rum and raisin,' said Nanna. 'And anyway, it's cold.'

'Put it in the oven for her,' my mother said quietly. 'It's not every day that Tatters dies.'

She was back and forth from the kitchen all after-noon. I offered to help with the washing-up. 'No fear. You'd only break everything.' She wiped a surface. 'My God, I'll be glad when this lot have gone. It's like a bloody Chinese takeaway.'

We took Nanna home in the evening. My father told me he'd been through Tatters' study, but if there was anything I particularly wanted, I should go upstairs and get it now.

Although I couldn't draw very well, I picked up his small box of watercolours and an old stamp album, which had stamps from Ascension, Malaya, Zanzibar, Montserrat and Tonga. I also took a book of Houseman's poems and a map of Birmingham in 1921. There was a lot of green on the map, even round Small Heath and King's Norton.

Before leaving the room, I lifted up the white lace cover from the safe and tried the door. It opened – heavily, but with ease. The pile of letters was still there. I made my decision, and stuffed them inside my anorak, put the other things in a paper bag and waited expectantly until we got home.

When I was sure that I couldn't be disturbed, I spread the letters out on my bed. I looked at the dates and placed them in order. They were written in German and about twenty years old. I stacked them neatly, and after a few minutes, even though they weren't yet in any particular order took one and slowly began to read.

Slobber chops wasn't very keen, but eventually allowed me to go to the Slythes' Christmas party. Mrs insisted. She even found a dress for me. I had to hack it around a bit, but beggars can't be choosers. And I spent a little of the money I've saved on war-paint. You should see my lips; red like a Venus fly-trap.

The Slythes' house is huge. A lot of panelling; also, an oak table with great robust legs, like a nigger's thighs. Paintings of small rural scenes. No portraits, but one of Dürer's hands.

I didn't know a lot of the people there. Marcus Hull was with a tall tart – thin as a rake, no meat on her and a lot younger than him. Men can't help it, I suppose. Dulcie

Slythe took me by the arm. It was as if she'd read my thoughts.

'That is his latest,' she told me, jerking her head towards the rake.

'He's not married then?'

She threw her head back and showed me a row of horse's teeth. 'Good heavens, no! Not him.'

I asked about the woman.

'Just one of his pieces. He usually gets through two or three a year. They're all keen enough. There's plenty of money about. Black Market, I shouldn't be surprised.' She hesitated.

'Which of the two worlds have you chosen then? The two worlds you're poised between,' she reminded me.

I said I was still wondering.

'Well don't take too long. That's my advice,' she said, 'or you may not have the choice. But I wouldn't be worried about Hull, my dear; he may have an eye for the ladies, but you are German. He's got political ambitions – you simply wouldn't do.'

Peter Slythe gave me a glass of something. He'd already had too much to drink and his cheeks were cherub red. Eyes like piss-holes in the snow. He said he was keen to 'exorcise any residual embarrassment and return our relationship to its former condition of easy familiarity'. He pointed out that man who had come to size Mrs Bacon's finger. His girlfriend was standing by, holding the glasses, looking bored and impatient. She'd really put it on with a towel, and was wearing the 'New Look'. Dulcie said, 'Name of Jade, and possibly pregnant – but not by him. The family are furious.' She looked like a sack of potatoes, or maybe the baby was showing.

'His parents would be delighted if someone took him out of her hands. Come on, I'll introduce you.'

To cut a long story short, Peter Slythe talked to Jade for a few minutes, and the jeweller asked me to see Fallen Angel *at the cinema in Stratford next week.*

His name is William; he's harmless and he's got a car. Be glad that I'll be enjoying myself, and let's not have any nonsense.

Nr. Stratford. December 27th, 1947.

About the only time we managed a family holiday was the time we went to Great Yarmouth the next half-term. My father had bought a second-hand blue Volkswagen camping van. The dashboard's expansive curve was too much for him. Clinging to it now were a whole new range of gadgets he could barely have contemplated in his wildest dreams. A coffee grinder and a toaster were rudely clamped onto the inviting plastic space alongside his more usual devices. He'd even had a socket installed to take a miniature black and white Japanese television, a souvenir from a visit to his favourite shop on the Tottenham Court Road.

'Mum'll like this,' I said hopefully, as we drove back from the showroom.

My father didn't reply. He checked the wing mirror and found Humphrey Lyttleton's programme on the radio. A few bars of the Duke's 'Long, Strong and Consecutive' ricocheted unnervingly around the van's abysmal interior.

'It's all very well,' my mother said, 'but if you think

I'm going to shit in that thing, you've got another think coming.'

She was standing half-way back in the van, near to its sliding side door, in a small cubicle built into the end of what we had all supposed to be a wardrobe. Beneath her a hole the size of a football had been cut out of a cream-coloured box, standing about two feet high. Barely discernible was a vivid blue liquid swilling around at the bottom. My mother peered into the hole with the reluctant look of a dentist about to approach a set of particularly rotten teeth.

'It smells now,' she said. 'Imagine what it'll be like when it's full.'

She looked at my father.

'Well I can't smell anything,' he replied.

'That's your bloody polyps for you. You can't smell anything.'

She looked around the rest of the van, probing every corner and concealed space. Occasionally she'd mutter, 'What's he bought this bloody thing for?' or 'He doesn't have to clean the ruddy thing,' but the small fridge softened her. So did the curtains, which were detachable and had to be neatly and ingeniously folded away after use. 'I'm still not using that toilet, though,' she eventually pronounced. 'I'll take my business elsewhere, thank you very much.'

The drive to Great Yarmouth a few weeks later was managed in persistent, driving rain.

'Dogs and cats,' my mother observed.

As usual, my father drove too fast, and when he had to suddenly slow down for a bend or quickly manoeuvre past another car, pots and pans would

153

habitually tumble out of the cupboard above the small stove. My mother had decided to pack her spare bras in the largest saucepan, and after it had crashed to the ground for the fifth time, she unbuckled the seatbelt and edged her way sourly to the back of the swaying van.

'There's nothing else for it.'

'What?' my father asked. He was more concerned with plotting a course through the misted windscreen he was now peering through. The fan was no longer working. In fact, it had never worked.

'I'll have to put them in the wardrobe.'

'What?'

'The bras, of course.'

'Do what you like.'

'You'll have to stop.'

'What.'

"You'll have to stop so I can unpack the wardrobe. The rest of my clothes are at the back. I'm not having my bras in with your stuff.'

'Why not?'

'I'm just not.'

My father pulled in at the next lay-by and took the chance to ask if anyone wanted a piece of toast or a mug of coffee. Whilst he was hunched over the dashboard, he also plugged in the miniature Japanese television. 'Good picture,' he said.

The screen was six inches square. I could see the blurred outline of a man in a dinner suit moving in sharp, rhythmic steps with a woman who seemed to be wearing a stiff, inflexible dress that ended in a perfect circle around her thighs.

154

'You don't like *Come Dancing*,' I replied.

'Good reception, though. Eh?'

'Well . . . it's all right . . .'

'You mother likes the dancing.'

'I bloody do not,' she shouted. 'Not on that thing, anyway. Who told you to pack these?' She held up a pair of blue y-fronts. 'They've still got that stain on them. There are some perfectly good white ones in your other drawer.'

'Too tight,' my father tried.

'Don't talk rubbish,' she snorted, and slid open the small window above the fridge before throwing the blue underpants on to the semi-grassed verge outside. 'The tramps can have these.'

After several rounds of burnt toast and a mug of cold coffee each, we continued on our journey. The rain was still washing down as we reached Great Yarmouth. It made a clattering echo on the van's roof, especially that part which was made of tough but reverberant plastic. Apparently, this housed a central portion which could be pushed skywards once we had stopped, allowing enough room for a stretcher with a tartan pattern to be clipped across the new space which had been created just beneath it. This was my bunk bed.

The campsite consisted of two square pebbledashed buildings set in a large field by now transformed into a large mudhole.

A small man wearing wellingtons and a green macintosh darted out of the first building as we approached. He introduced himself as 'Mr Sprig, the proud proprietor of Camp Yarmouth', with 'the best facilities this side of Lowestoft'. He was neatly groomed with an impeccably sharp parting. Although my mother had always been very particular about partings, she still inspected him thoroughly from her passenger seat, several feet above.

He told my father that as it was now getting dark, there was no need to pay until the morning. With that, he gave a little smile and hopped around to the other side of the van. He called back over his shoulder, 'I don't even have to duck to get under this,' and raised the red and white striped pole which had barred our entrance. On the way up, it gave off a mechanical screech. We trundled slowly past Mr Sprig, who was still smiling. My mother shot him a look of dark, intense menace. Even the seemingly irrepressible Mr Sprig withered slightly as the barrier clanked down behind us.

Once inside Camp Yarmouth I peered through the windows on either side of the van. Our holiday home for the next week was smeared out before me in all four directions. It was still pouring, six-inch nails picked out from the dark in the Volkswagen's head-lamps. I could make out a huddled collection of sodden tents, and rather fewer camping vans spotted randomly over a brown morasse about the size of a cricket field. Some of the tents seemed to be on the point of collapse, their canvasses buckling under the weight of water which had made strange indentations in what should have been smooth slopes of fabric. As we sailed by, the other pebbledashed building now showed itself to be a small café on one side, with red formica tables arranged in three rows of five. It was just closing, and the last customers were about to make a dash for their tents, about two hundred yards away. One had a brown paper bag which he used to cover his head against the lashing. Another used a copy of the *Daily Mirror* which gradually came apart and unravelled into the mud as he started to run.

There were two other doors with signs above them reading 'Gentlemen' and 'Ladies'. A middle-aged man wearing a vest and shorts was going through the first, a towel slung purposefully over his shoulder.

My mother insisted we find a space as near to the bathroom as possible. She had made no compromises about the van's chemical toilet, and once said that she'd come all the way to England 'to get away from that sort of thing'.

As my father jolted us towards the nearest available space, I caught a glimpse of the North Sea at the extreme corner of the camp. We must have been on top of a cliff. I wondered how far it was to Germany. A small ship was bucking on the corrugated waves. We turned sharply and came to a stop. Immediately, the pots and pans clattered to the floor again in one final metallic hail.

I could see Mr Sprig at the flagpole outside his office, struggling to take down the Union Jack.

My mother and father barely said a word beyond what was necessary to make the van ready for sleeping. We swayed around the centre of the vehicle, bumping into each other, finally raising the roof and getting the tartan stretcher in position. I climbed up, and my mother said, 'That's you out of the way, anyway.' Then she put all the curtains up, pushed past my father and slid gracelessly into her own sleeping bag on the double bed at the back of the van. She took a hairnet, a small jellied eel and a jar of pickled gherkins out of her overnight bag. My father was crouched over the dashboard watching *Danger Man*. After a few minutes, my mother turned her light off. My father put some earplugs into a socket on the side of the television, and continued to watch. I lay on my back several feet above them both, wedged between two metal poles, unable to move. The rain was spitting only a few inches away from my head. Condensation was already running down the inside of the plastic roof above me. A surreal, greyish glow lit up the front of the van.

I eventually fell asleep out of exhaustion. The condensation had gathered to a steady trickle of icy water which ran into my face. The tartan stretcher held me rigidly in place so that it was all I could manage to turn even slightly away from this discomfort.

In the morning, I was woken by the smell of burning toast. I peered over the side of the 'bed' to see my father scraping charcoal from a buckled black rectangle out of the window and on to the mud and tufts of grass outside. The curtains had been taken down; the sun was shining.

Determined to see things through, he crammed what was left of the mutilated bread into his mouth and announced he was going to get a paper. Before he set off to find the nearest newsagent, I asked him where my mother was. He said she'd complained of being bitten by something during the night, and had gone off 'in a bit of a huff'. Things had obviously not been going well that morning. I decided to explore the campsite, and after dressing on the floor of the van to avoid spying from the outside, I stepped out onto the sticky ground and headed towards the café where most of the campers appeared to be. Seagulls caught the breeze and glided effortlessly above me; there was a smell of savoury rust in the air. Even though the sun was up, a sharp wind cut across Mr Sprigs' field. I noticed that the flag was flapping manically over his office.

As I walked towards the café, I saw that the other campers were huddled together in front of the toilet block. Some were still carrying towels and small, puffy toiletry bags, but others were simply shuffling about, clearly fixed on something that was happening right in front of the Ladies'.

I pushed through the crowd to see what the fuss was all about. I saw my mother on the concreted area immediately in front of the block. She was washing herself from an isolated tap; a pipe led back to the pebbledashed wall about a yard to the left of the entrance. She was wearing no clothes and was lathering herself with a block of Imperial Leather that Nanna had given her for Christmas two years ago. Occasionally, she would say something to whoever was standing nearest to her. This accounted for the slow movement of the crowd, anxious to avoid being still yet remain within earshot.

'Smashing soap this – not that you need the bubbles of course,' she was saying, between vigorous strokes down her left leg. 'Always queues – why bother waiting? – see those bites – mosquitoes, I reckon.

Little buggers.' Now she was doing the small of her back. 'Don't mind me – I'm sure you've all seen it before – I've not got anything to be ashamed of, you know.' Now she was working away at her buttocks, pushing the flesh around and creating a thin layer of soap which she massaged with a circular movement of her hand. 'During the war, I saw a man bitten by a snake – his balls came up like pumpkins . . .'

Nobody was saying much.

Eventually, she finished and slipped on her pink dressing-gown. Then she padded resolutely back towards the van. I slipped into the Gents' toilet, stood in front of the first available urinal, stared at the damp khaki concrete in front of me and closed my eyes.

I'm not sure whether my father knew about the event. He seemed unconcerned by the staring that my mother inevitably attracted afterwards, and as it was the beginning of a new cricket season, he had a lot on his mind.

The rest of the week passed without discomfort. Occasionally, when it wasn't raining, we went for walks on the beach, though it was too cold to go swimming. Some of the campers were often in the sea despite the weather, and my mother dismissed them as 'barmy', or in one particular case, 'fat enough not to let it worry him'.

After the incident outside the Ladies' toilets, she had become quiet, though oddly preoccupied. My mother's uncharacteristic stillness suggested that she was restless. I found myself willing a cruel or sharp word from her, though none actually came. Once I noticed that she was looking towards the sea, perhaps at some point beyond. Her eyes were still and intense, a deep black, fixed on something that only she could see. Her motionlessness made me uncomfortable. I thought about the letters, mostly unopened and lying where I knew she wouldn't find them – in her wardrobe, underneath the neat pile of nearly-new handbags that had been discarded over the years.

'Time to clean the fridge,' she suddenly said towards the end of the week, and set off towards the back of the van. There was now only an apple, two carrots, some jellied pork and a jar of beetroot perched on the middle shelf. Even the can of Carnation had been finished. Nothing could have changed; she'd only 'cleaned through' a couple of hours ago. It was the fourth time that day she'd been to the fridge. My father was still working through last Sunday's papers. Finally putting them down, he looked anxiously around, and said, 'Where's your mother?'

On the last day, we decided to go shopping in the town. We settled with Mr Sprigs, who raised the barrier for us. This time he didn't make a joke, although my mother was crumpled up in her seat, lost in thought. Despite the uncertain weather, the camp was steadily filling up. 'Bloody fools,' my mother said. Then she opened a bag of eucalyptus mints she'd been saving from the previous summer.

We drove around the centre of Great Yarmouth looking for a parking space for about twenty minutes. 'Let's just go home. I've had enough of this,' my mother snapped. My father pretended not to hear. He turned the van into the High Street and manoeuvred it towards the entrance of a multi-storey car park.

'Don't be daft. We won't fit in there. We're too bloody high.'

My father took no notice. He tore a ticket from the small box at the entrance, and edged the van up the concrete ramp. We made it on to the first level, but as we steered towards the upward spiral leading to the next one, the van suddenly and unaccountably stalled. My father hissed 'Bugger' under his breath, and turned the key in the ignition. No matter how hard he tried to accelerate, he could only move the vehicle a few inches before a splintering, ripping noise came from the top. Wedged tight, the upper section of the Volkswagen was gradually being torn away from the main body.

'Bugger,' he said again, more loudly this time. I looked out of the rear window and saw clouds of grey smoke filling the car park. There was a smell of scorching rubber and a sound of horns.

'You bloody fool,' my mother finally said. 'Serves you right.' Then she started to laugh. Several days of near inertia evaporated as her eyes closed and the tears trickled down her cheeks. My father slumped over the steering wheel, his face sheepish and impatient.

Then, the van door was opened and my father was pulled out on to the ground. A large man with shoulder-length hair and sideboards the size and shape of small hedgehogs was standing over him.

'Think it's funny, do you? How the hell am I going to get out? You're blocking me. Moron.'

'Oh . . . bugger off . . .' my father said.

The large man picked my father up by his shirt-collar and threw him down again. I saw that his chin was bleeding and he had turned a deathly pale. His attacker was walking threateningly forwards, pushing up his sleeves like they always do. From nowhere, my mother was on his back with her legs around the man's waist. Her arms were flailing like windmills and he stopped advancing, more surprised than hurt. One of her arms stopped rotating and she jabbed her large diamond solitaire ring into his eye. Her other arm was thumping the side of his head. He started to buck like an enraged bull, but my mother clung on for quite a while, continuing her assault all the time, before eventually being thrown off. Several other drivers now appeared from their cars. The man's moment had gone, and he staggered back to his Chrysler Princess, shouting insults at my mother, before reversing aimlessly off into the gloom of the car park, back where he had just come from.

Someone advised my father to let down the tyres, so as to reduce the van's height, and then to drive carefully out.

Nobody said anything very much on the way home, but I couldn't exorcise the image of my mother from my mind. It was not what she'd done, although that had been something in itself. Whilst she was attacking the man, her eyes had taken on the same black intensity I'd noticed when she was looking out across the sea a few days before. Even my father knew something was up. It was Saturday afternoon and the radio was left dead.

PART TWO

– I –

Initially, I was shocked when my mother went into hospital.

It wasn't that the idea of death was unfamiliar, because Mother had always surrounded herself with people who were either close to it or just perpetually ill. And then there were Aunty Betty and Mrs Frings, both of whom lived in a world beyond ours, and not quite in the next.

I remembered that Aunty Bernie had died when I was five years old – of cancer. Once, I'd locked myself in her toilet. She'd left me fifty pounds in her will. I always wondered whether Aunty Bernie was really a man.

Last year, and some time since I'd found the letters, Herr Klink had committed suicide. He'd retired and sold the butcher's shop, and mother said he'd just got weary of the doctor's daily visits to dress his war wound. 'That leg was still weeping, thirty years after the bloody war ended,' she said. 'It still oozed like a rubber tree.' Herr Klink had taken the gun he'd often used for shooting bolts through cows' heads, and put one through his own.

There were others, and I was beginning to realise that there was more to dying than *Thunderball* had suggested. Being skewered to a palm tree by a dart from an underwater gun or eaten alive by sharks in a swimming pool took on a kind of spectacular edge that the messy reality lacked.

Tatters' death had, in retrospect, acquired a kind of mystical patterning. One Saturday, he'd stopped going to watch Birmingham play.

'I don't really feel up it,' he said.

'I'm not sure any of us do,' my father joked, 'but there we are, always going back for more punishment.' His jokes were as rare as happiness, but when they arrived, they usually carried the stamp of a weary but good-natured pessimism. He made dejection palatable.

This joke, however, was a waste.

There was something in Tatters' eyes that declared a realisation that his time was up, or at least would be, sooner rather than later. Crumpled white bags of toffee were turning up untouched all over the flat, Nanna didn't even bother opening the stout for his Saturday lunches any more, and he took to sitting in his armchair, dozing quietly, for hours at a time.

One night, as his skin went yellow, the doctor said he couldn't pay a call because it was Sunday. Tatters soiled himself every night for a week, and Nanna could only watch in helpless disbelief as the washing piled up.

'She's a tough old vulture,' my mother said, 'but

you've got to feel sorry for her. Maybe she'd like some of that risotto from Sainsbury's.'

By the time Tatters was finally taken to hospital, and the doctors said he had poisoned blood, he was both yellow and purple. He ripped out all the plastic tubes that had been inserted into the porcelain surface of his shiny, translucent skin and thrashed about like a fish out of water. He never recognised me when I came to see him, but did ask who'd scored.

'Bridges,' I lied, 'Barry Bridges.'

The settled him. 'I thought so.'

An hour later, he was dead.

'Poor old sod,' Mother said. 'I suppose Her Ladyship wants me to do the funeral. I'll be buggered if I will.' But, of course, she did, even down to the soggy saltsticks.

Despite all these thoughts, Mother was, after all, only going into hospital. She had been getting headaches for several weeks, and her overpowering, demonic energy had been ebbing away. She began to bump into furniture without spray-wiping it afterwards. The telephone accumulated greasy smudges around the earpice.

Casually, she started to break things. This was an alarming development as she always hoarded objects with the bloodyminded tenacity of a magpie. A particularly cherished loss was an early 1950s tea-caddy filled with hamster food and confidentially labelled 'Sugar', even though my hamster had never been replaced since her ethereal, explosive end several years earlier.

My father knew something was up when he came home one evening to find my mother in bed. On his way through the kitchen, he'd noticed three shattered German mustard pots on the floor. She'd been collecting these for years, treating each pot like a beaker, and scouring every one clean after the mustard was finished so that we could drink from them.

'Smashing,' she'd say, 'who needs to buy glasses when you can get these for free?'

Neither my father nor I liked mustard, and we didn't know where it went, but she'd amassed thirty-seven 'beakers' when he discovered the breakages.

This was the time to call Dr Powell-Tuck.

He'd burned my warts off a year ago. Surely if he could get rid of them he wouldn't have any trouble with a headache.

I went away on holiday to Abersoch with Mark Perkins and his family while things were sorted out.

No doubt action should have been taken earlier. My father was spending a lot of time at the office then and was also, I now suspect, discreetly enjoying the calm that came with my mother's gradual emasculation. She was more preoccupied with not falling down and bumping into things than with finding ingenious methods of closing down his little avenues of pleasure.

I recognised the signs and detected a slightly jaunty air, carefully concealed underneath a frowning concern. Making the most of it, I persuaded him to buy me *John Buchan's Pictorial History of Football* and a floral-patterned cotton shirt (with tie) to take with me to Wales.

We were both breathing free and easy.

Abersoch was a disaster. I fell out of a red sailing boat when we went fishing, argued with Mark Perkins about everything and spilt tea over my new shirt. I broke one of Mr Perkins' golf clubs on the local seaside course. It was my first game of golf and I took nineteen on the first hole. When we arrived back at the rented bungalow, Mrs Perkins told me that my father had telephoned with the news that my mother was about to go into hospital. He thought it best that I should return home immediately. Nobody stood in my way.

Mr Perkins gave me a list of the stations my train would be passing through on the way back to Birmingham, in addition to a note about the three changes I would have to make. It was my first solo train journey, and the only time I'd been more than a few miles by rail. I carefully ticked off each station as we came to it, driven to near panic at the prospect of becoming lost.

It was a hot day. The small diesel rattled alongside ribbons of yellow beaches for the first hour or so, before ducking east towards the Midlands. The sun filled my swaying carriage, blinding eyes and causing passengers to squint. It was crowded with garish, colourful holiday-makers. Minutes crawled past.

I had a copy of *Beau Geste* which my mother had

given me as part of my birthday present the previous year. I'd only taken it to Abersoch to please her, and it was still unopened. Reading seemed impossible. I was juggling with the station names, keeping an eye on my luggage and trying to remain remote and inconspicuous at the same time. A balding, fat man with a gold watch-chain and round wire-rimmed spectacles always seemed to be looking at me. At least I wasn't wearing lederhosen.

I sat with heavy bubbles of sweat sliding down my body, discovering obscure folds and creases in my skin. I wondered who else knew about them, and might disapprove. I thought about how slowly the time was passing. As each moment came and went, I wondered about its unique nature, never to be repeated again. All those unique moments, happening one after the other, and then gone for ever.

The rhythm of the train took up with my mind, each sleepered clatter representing one of those lost, precious incidents.

And now it is gone. And now it is gone.

The tracks ate time up.

The only way to make sense of it all was to drag the past around so that the present never simply disappeared. Then we would always have something to fall back on, like my mother's tea-caddy. I remembered *Beau Geste* and my father's collection of Coventry Speedway programmes. I supposed that when something in your past simply wouldn't do, you just rejected it and manufactured a different, more convenient history. Even if you changed your past, weren't you reacting to it? It still influenced you and

determined how you behaved. Mother's letters to
Rainer revealed a different person all those years ago.
She'd walked away from that character and jettisoned
everything about her previous self. That was her past's
legacy. Maybe I was about to turn my back on her in
the same way she'd done with Rainer and her own
parents. Were those letters now a part of my own past
which I also couldn't ignore?

Only when there was no future would the past
relinquish its hold.

I recalled a story we'd read at school about time
coming to an end. There'd been a kind of cosmic
clock, counting down units until the end of the
universe. A computer had picked up signals from
outer space . . .

96,688,365,498,695
96,688,365,498,694
96,688,365,498,693 . . .

There was a hypnotic pleasure in the whole thing.

I worried about the magnitude of the forces I'd been
contemplating, and decided there was still time to start
Beau Geste before the final change at Wolverhampton,
where the sky had become a slate-grey and all the
people seemed to be old and unhappy. They wore
crimson on their blotchy faces.

My father met me at Birmingham New Street Station.
I could tell that things weren't right as he was wearing
a dark suit, a long-forgotten cravat and a pair of
maroon slippers. In the car on the way to the hospital

he told me that my mother had had 'a number of dizzy spells and was having difficulty holding her food down'. There was a fearful distance from the actuality of the event in his mechanical use of Dr Powell-Tuck's words. He had barely coped with the three shattered mustard pots.

Feeling somehow responsible, though, he gamely tried to prepare me by saying that she 'had a tumour on her brain', and more quietly, 'inside her head', to ensure I'd understood completely. He attempted to lighten the information by saying that when they'd first gone to the hospital and seen the X-rays, my mother had said, 'My God – it's the size of a bloody satsuma. Bet they don't get many like that in this place.'

Nothing he said prepared me for the dreadful sight of her in the wheelchair. My mother barely recognised me. She was desperately thin. A foamy dribble escaped from her lips. The unhinged head lolled to one side, its expression never changing, eyes half-open but never blinking. Someone had taken out her false front teeth in case she swallowed them. The rest of her body was simply useless, a puppet with cut strings. Thin legs awkwardly crossed on the wheelchair's footrests, hair sprouting untidily from disregarded ducts. Matchstick arms resting redundantly, modestly, on her lap. Her skin had become coarse and obscurely stained with yellow as though lightly garnished with pale custard. Her usually buoyant cheeks were now sunk beneath an anarchic crazy-paving of burst blood vessels. She had the scrawny neck of a turkey.

My father stood behind the wheelchair, scar-lipped and serious. I couldn't say anything, not even that I'd started *Beau Geste*.

That evening, I looked up 'Tumour' in *Black's Medical Dictionary*, also bought by my father on the same day that he'd become engaged to my mother. 'He was so excited they could have sold him anything,' I remembered her telling me. 'Bloody fool.'

'Tuiarameia' was a rodent disease.

I was stuck by:

(i) 'TUMOURA means literally any swelling . . .'

(ii) 'MALIGNANT TUMOURS of imperfect structure resembling the cells of skin, mucous membranes of secreting glands, are known generally as CANCERS . . .'

(iii) '*Treatment*: the treatment of tumours is, in general, its removal by operation. If a tumour is malignant, or if there is any doubt as to its character, an operation should be performed at the earliest possible opportunity.'

I thought of my mother's satsuma-sized cellular structure. The swelling didn't show on the outside, so it must be pushing the other way, against her brain, shoving it all out of shape, stopping her blood moving round. No wonder she wasn't bothering with the spray-wipe.

As we left the hospital, my father and I looked hopelessly at each other. In some ways, it was the closest thing to intimacy we'd ever achieved – even though this was merely a shared and desolate anxiety. I tried to look on the bright side, and the glory to be had in reclaiming the kitchen grill for cooking purposes. I concentrated on being able to choose my own clothes each day, to hide the lederhosen, and not have to search for the fuses for the electric fire.

The car park was next to the waste ground which led to the pipes where the boy from next door but seven had fallen several years ago. They still hissed and steamed menacingly, and the barbed-wire surround had gone rusty. I no longer wondered whether it was worth throwing myself on them. I was either growing up or going off Sherbet Fountains.

You have not written, Rainer. Why not? It has been over three weeks since I heard a word from you. You talked about Space, Time and Strindberg. Don't forget that Stendhal said he would rather his wife stab him twice a year than be greeted every evening with a sour face.

If it's any consolation, Fallen Angel *was melodramatic and obvious. I fell asleep. Who wants to see sickly suburban housewives and waitresses being murdered?*

I miss your letters, Rainer. And you. What more do you want me to say? And you were right about Bacon; no more envelopes.

Never mind. Just write.

Nr. Stratford. January 20th, 1948.

— 2 —

'Any longer and the tumour would have caused irreparable damage,' Dr Dodds cheerfully told my father and I. Like all doctors, he was washing his hands and smelt of chalk. 'The operation will still be dangerous. As it is, things are touch and go . . .' Somehow, I felt as if I should be grateful.

With my mother away in hospital, a strange peace fell over the house. Out of respect, we left the cleaning fluids in the grill and decided instead to fry the best quality bacon my father bought from Rackham's Food Hall. He always loosed himself on the delicatessens of Birmingham at times of independence, and I made a silent bet with myself that before the week was out he would not only abandon drip-dries but also rediscover Morgan's Rum Hair Pomade.

He was still concerned and talked of the tumour as a 'shocking business', but there was also a carefree relief in his behaviour, permitted because he wasn't actually responsible for the circumstances which had led to this domestic respite.

I supposed that he loved my mother. He certainly

couldn't ignore her. Over the years she'd managed to insinuate herself with the subtlety of a slide trombonist.

Even now she was still strongly present. We carefully puffed cushions back into shape after sitting on them, wiped surfaces clean after use, shined taps, dried plugs, dusted telephones, and always wound the flex from the Hoover back in the right way.

Despite the persevering image of my disconnected mother, our daily routine was fluent and my father in good spirits. There were other factors which contributed to his buoyancy, and as we were often together these gradually made themselves apparent. It was like finding a station on the radio that you always knew was 'there', but had never really listened for.

In other ways, normal life had been disrupted for several months. The IRA had bombed a pub in Birmingham and, just up the road, had demolished a wing of the local Conservative Club Headquarters. I could remember the blast because it caused the needle playing across my copy of The Who's *Quadrophenia* to slip. Afterwards, it would always stick on '5:15'.

A state of emergency had been declared when coal supplies were cut by a miners' overtime ban. My mother had called the Arabs 'wogs' when they cut oil supplies to the West. She had excelled in the crisis, and we had more stockpiled candles than anyone else in the road. Gleefully, she'd anticipated each blackout and a chart went up in the kitchen drawing attention to the savings on fuel bills. Once, I was sent up the road with several candles for Aunty Betty, because 'the poor soul can't get to the shops'. But Mrs Frings was not to get any on account of her hallucinations: 'If she believes in those silly sods in the bushes, let one of them buy the bloody things.'

All this led to the three-day week, and this was what delighted my father. Business came to a virtual standstill, and he could just make rings without the tiresome chore of dealing with other people and having to sell them at a profit. Soon, he was pottering around the office enjoying the security of absolute paralysis. The principle was the only thing that mattered to him – he only played at reality. In particular, he adored the postal strike. No bills arrived for several weeks. 'Lovely,' he'd say every morning. 'No post. Not a bloody sausage. It's going to take the bank months to sort this one out.'

Maybe it had been the happiest year in my father's life: IRA bombs, electricity cuts, postal strikes and now my mother's satsuma; all combined to create an incredible release from claustrophobic routines. A fantasy world where nobody expected anything of him. He simply tinkered with existence.

Birmingham were playing Arsenal in the FA Cup. As usual, my father drove to the ground avoiding all the main roads, criss-crossing through a tangle of side streets until we arrived about ten minutes before the kick-off.

There was a regularity about all our visits to watch football. We had a car-park ticket and always parked in the same space. Our season ticket entitled us to the same seats every week, even for cup games. We sat in the middle of the stand, just above the director's box, in what my mother would have called 'the swanky seats'.

The same people sat around us. Esmond, who used to keep wicket for Warwickshire; his fingertips were bent backwards from repeated catching of cricket balls. The Mucklows, who all had orange hair, and only came, it seemed to me, to shout abuse at the Birmingham players. They weren't very good, but it was somehow unfair. My father was often on the point of telling them to be quiet, but never quite managed it. Once, just after Tatters had died, Mr Mucklow had snorted chummily, 'Where's the old man, then?'

'Dead,' I said.

That kept him quiet for a week or so, but it wasn't long before he was shouting again.

A very fat man with inflated, carbuncular cheeks sat in the press box two rows behind us, where the journalists' typewriters kept up a constant chatter. I was fascinated by the size of his face. He also stopped coming after a while.

The ground was full; 55,000 people were swelling it with a barrage of uncoordinated sound. A Salvation Army band was trying to make itself heard down on the pitch. Recently, the club had taken to using a group of cheerleaders to provide the pre-match entertainment. The choice of the Salvation Army was clearly to mark the dignity of this occasion.

Mr Mucklow leant forward and tapped my father on the shoulder. 'Could be an upset tonight, eh?'

My father gave his thin, startled grin. 'We'll see,' he nodded.

Birmingham were in the Second Division. As far as I could tell, they always had been. Neither had they ever won the cup. Success was not destined for the team and its supporters. Both thrived on cheerful non-achievement. A part of my mother would have approved. She was always saying how nothing really mattered. 'We all go the same way in the end,' she often told me.

The Arsenal players seemed to outnumber the Birmingham team. They also looked bigger. I put it down to the hooped socks. They didn't allow us to touch the ball for the first fifteen minutes and scored an easy goal.

'I'm not watching this,' my father said.

What chance have we got, I thought. One of our players has a low pulse rate and another has to take his teeth out before every game.

At half-time, my father took out his miniature Russian radio, put the earpiece in and listened to the scores from other games. Although they would also be shown on a large black scoreboard in the corner of the ground, he liked to be ahead of everyone else.

'Bloody thing,' he snapped, moving the radio round in the palm of his hand, trying to get good reception.

I shuffled closer to him and half whispered in his

other ear. 'It might be the wax – clogging up the earpiece.'

He took it out and gave it a good clean with the end of a bent paper clip he always kept in his wallet. The earpiece went back in. 'Villa are losing,' he smiled. 'Bastards.'

In the second half, Birmingham scored two goals. 'Lucky, lucky so-and-sos,' yelled Mr Mucklow. The giant clock next to the scoreboard only had a minute hand, and was meant to synchronise with playing time on the pitch. It never did, and was now moving in the wrong direction. Time was running backwards.

After the game, and in the spirit of euphoria, my father bought me a hotdog.

'Don't be sick again,' he warned, remembering what had happened when we'd gone to Leicester.

'I was still picking the stuff out of the carpet two weeks later,' my mother had said.

We drove home, and my father said goodnight before disappearing downstairs to do some work. It wasn't long before Earl Hines' 'Fat Babes' was boomeranging around the kitchen. I thought I heard the grill go on.

The first weekend by ourselves I went with him to the office, still at a glorious standstill. Nobody was there apart from Old Albert who sometimes came in on Saturdays to finish a job he'd been too slow to complete on Friday. His fingers were stained nicotine-yellow, a different kind of yellow from my mother's colouring.

He asked after her.

'Much the same,' my father replied. 'They're doing all they can.'

'When's the operation?'

'Tuesday or Wednesday, I think.'

'Still, they can do wonderful things these days. My sister, Violet, she had some lumps removed only last year. Wonderful things.'

I wondered whether he meant the operations or the growth, and thought of my father's nasal polyps, which meant he couldn't smell or taste anything. It was just as well with my mother's cooking.

I said, 'Yes.'

My father was busy checking the alarm system. It had never worked properly since Tatters used to accidentally set it off every Saturday morning.

The conversation with Old Albert was carried out between long sighs, averted eyes and nodded heads.

'They can even put a monkey's heart in a human being, you know.' Albert was warming up.

'I shouldn't think it will be necessary though, do you?'

Neither Albert or myself were sure this was a joke.

The rest of the morning went quickly. My father told me about inflation and the 17.1% rise in the Retail Price Index, both of which made buying gold and price-setting impossible to gauge. We immersed ourselves in money he didn't possess. He told me about 'cash flow' and how to make the movement of money around the business easier. He'd started up several different bank accounts which all handled essentially the same financial capital.

'As long as the banks don't find out who owns all these accounts, it will always seem as if we've got more money than we really have,' he enthused. Some accounts had exotic names like Paradise Investments and Utopian Accounts, while others were more utilitarian: BJM and Solitaire Diamonds. He delighted in explaining how the rapid transfer of funds from one account to the next, supplemented by the carefully timed writing of cheques, should ensure that, as far as the banks were concerned, there was an apparently fluid, continuous supply of money.

For extra pocket money I had learnt how to enter figures into the business' financial ledgers and Day Book. I spent an hour with the latest clutch of invoices from people like Peplow's of Worcester and Knowle Horologists. It was difficult to think that – somehow – all this amounted to a house, two cars, a comfortable living for three people and a growing collection of jazz cassettes.

He spent the last part of the morning weighing diamonds on an Oertling balance and then sorting them into different sizes. He picked each one up in a pair of stainless-steel tweezers and scrutinised it through a conical eyeglass which he squeezed into a puckered eye-socket. The work was done quickly and expertly, and he'd soon arranged several small piles. Then, he subdivided them into tens and folded them neatly into packets of greaseproof paper.

Whilst he was doing this, I wrote a speedway report for him, which would also give me extra pocket money. It would be sent to *The Speedway Star* and printed in the next edition. Even under my father's name, I thrilled to see my own phrases on the page: 'Boocock found enough grip to drive round him on the outside,' and 'Though quickly out of the tapes, it was clear that Cotterell would be pressed all the way by the energetic Swede if he wanted his maximum.' Sometimes there was an opportunity for invention: 'Lightfoot pressured him on the inside, and the hapless Dane was sent spinning to the fence in a shower of shale and dirt.'

'You can't say that,' my father said, just before we left.

'Why not?'

'It's too flowery. Too ornamental. Too many words.'

'Well – I like it.'

'You won't be told, will you.' But he was smiling, and I knew he wouldn't change it.

By the time we went to visit my mother on the way home, the weather had turned. Even for early summer it was bracing, and the sun was struggling to push through the purplish, cloying smog that wafted from the city. I could just make out the edges of a pale, creamy disc high in the sky, which had no real effect other than making my father shield his eyes whenever he threw the Mini in a particular direction.

He'd just had a new cassette player installed and put on Ben Webster playing 'In a Mellow Tone'. There was little talk. The resonant tenor sax filled the small car with an optimistic, honeyed mood of well-being.

It was some time before I realised that again we weren't driving home the usual way. I mentioned it, and my father's face became distracted and he started to bite the loose skin at the top of his fingers. He always did this when he was anxious. He sounded unconvincing; 'Just got to drop some stuff in at the polisher's.'

'But there isn't any polishing. You told me. And besides, Maureen doesn't live out here.'

We were now driving around a series of unfamiliar roads and small avenues in a scruffy suburb to the south of Birmingham.

'This is a different polisher. Maureen's not doing this batch.'

Now he was hunched over the wheel, pretending to look as if he didn't know where he was going.

'I think it's round here somewhere,' he said, bringing the car to a stop in an anonymous and conveniently discreet backstreet. 'Wait here – I won't be a tick.'

It was a routine he'd practiced before, but this time I wasn't in the mood to ignore it. I sat alone for the next few minutes. I listened to the distant pounding of traffic from the main road.

I knew where my father was. I'd known for two years that he was having an affair with an Irish woman called Olive. Last Christmas, my mother had given him a jar of stuffed olives as his only present. It had been a mischievous tease which cheapened the outrage. We'd all laughed. My father even said, 'Thank you.' Scandals are only really effective when they're secretive. With my mother, they were about as discreet as the Shipping Forecast.

I'd met Olive once. In a moment of good-natured stupidity, my father had given her a job at the office. She had long peroxide-blonde hair which looked as if it had been collected from a platoon of Barbie dolls. There was a lot of turquoise eye make-up and an overpowering smell of sweet perfume. When she spoke, her words were empty and without expression, as pleasant and substantial as tinned custard. Even I knew she was a tart. 'A tart with a heart,' Uncle Lance had called her. But he had said it with a resigned shake of his dwarfish head.

My father maintained that he had stopped seeing her, but my mother was convinced of several things:

(i) that he still saw her

(ii) that he'd bought a house for her; 'only a terraced house, and I bet it's filthy'

(iii) that he'd somehow found employment for her two children

(iv) that 'the bloody Irish should sod off back to their own country if they're so bloody proud of it'

(v) that the original story – Olive was the wife of a friend killed during the war, and my father had promised to look after her – was actually 'a pile of horseshit'.

But Olive hadn't interfered with my mother's life for several months, and the matter had lain dormant. Waiting for my father, I judged him and ejected Ben Webster. If there was ever a time for Sonny Rollins, this was it.

On the way home, he knew something had

changed. He'd only been out of the car for ten minutes, but I wouldn't even take fish and chips from him. I thought of my mother lying in her hospital bed, limp and quite useless, and grew angry.

My father played a *Goon Show* cassette. It was the one with a character wearing a tin of shoe polish on his head.

'He says he always wears one on Wednesdays.'

'But it's Thursday today.'

'Oh, I feel such a fool,' replies the first character.

I knew how he felt and carefully avoided a smile.

Aunty Betty was already at the hospital by the time we arrived. Her crutches were leant against the bed-side, her hands considerately cradling my mother's meagre palm. There was a box of chocolates from Nanna on the bedside table. It was a present as maliciously useful as a pair of running spikes would have been to Aunty Betty. She was about to start reading from The New English Bible. She fumbled with her spectacles, which were dangling from a brown cord looped around her neck.

'Now, my dear. I'll take as my text a little from the Corinthians.' Aunty Betty cleared her throat. 'Chapter 1. And I'll start to read at verse 12.'

She had an overripe, plummy voice, the sort you associate with 1940s radio announcers. She read slowly and deliberately with great conviction. My mother remained spreadeagled across the bed. Even a reassuring grimace was well out of her range.

'Now if this is what we proclaim, that Christ was raised from the dead, how can some of you say there is no resurrection of the dead?'

Aunty Betty glanced up. For a moment she looked uncertain, but then she gathered herself up again.

'If there be no resurrection, then Christ was not raised; and if Christ was not raised, then our gospel is null and void, and so is your faith . . .'

Her voice had swelled to a sweeping evangelical certainty. She was instinctively moving her hand up and down in time to some unconsciously imposed beat. As she did so, she took my mother's inanimate arm and thumped it repeatedly against the side of the bed.

'. . . But the truth is,' she continued, 'Christ *was* raised to life – the first fruits of the harvest of the dead.'

One of the nurses came over to where my father and I were watching the scene.

'She's better today,' she smiled sweetly. 'We even got some pureed carrots down her.'

'Good,' my father said, without really understanding why.

'I think she was trying to smile this morning. Some things seem to be getting through.'

'Has she said . . . anything? Spoken. At all?' he tried, rather automatically. My father was staring blankly ahead. The question was drowned out, however.

'. . . Again, where are those who receive baptism on behalf of the dead? Why should they do this? If the

189

dead are not raised to life at all, what do they mean by being baptised on their behalf?'

Everybody in the ward turned round, wondering if the final question was in any way relevant to them. Aunty Betty stopped to take a breath. The reading was clearly drawing to some sort of climax and her cheeks were crimson-pink with the effort.

'She means well,' the nurse whispered, nodding her head and bringing her teeth together in something that wasn't quite a smile.

At that moment, a thin but unmistakable orange trickle wormed its way out of my mother's mouth. It quickly became a slow, thickening torrent and the nurse strode to her side. She was near shouting. 'You're deliberately being sick, aren't you? That's the second time today. This is no accident, is it? We'll only have to start again, you know. And then it's the funnel – and we don't want that, do we . . . ?'

'But you may ask,' thundered Aunty Betty, 'how are the dead raised? In what kind of body? How foolish! The seed you sow does not come to life unless it has first died . . .'

When the nurse had finished cleaning the mess from my mother's plastic bib, I saw her lips contriving a faint grin.

Nurse Binns – I'd noticed her name label – wrung the orange mush out of her cloth. She came over again just as Aunty Betty was winding up. 'This perishable being must be clothed with the imperishable, and what is mortal must be clothed with immortality . . .'

'There is one thing. It's probably not worth mentioning, but . . .'

My father looked mildly interested, as if something in the sports pages had momentarily taken his fancy.

Nurse Binns, clearly feeling that she really did have something important to say, started again: 'We found a photograph under her pillow. Whenever we look at it . . . which we have to . . . I mean when we change the bed . . . and it seems as if we might be about to take it away . . . well, you can just tell. She gets upset.'

My father, head down, nodding in measured bursts, was obviously being invited to enquire about the photograph. She didn't know him. He wouldn't ask, and Nurse Binns was reluctant to go on. 'It's rather delicate . . .' She whispered in the kind of self-important way that implied the desire to be heard.

My father, stranded in the aisle between the beds, was statuesque and uncomprehending. Nurse Binns said, 'Maybe not in front of your son . . .' and tugged him towards a screen.

I strained to hear what she was saying, but anything I might have heard was immediately engulfed by the waves of impenetrable belief now washing over my mother's bedside.

'Therefore, my beloved brothers, stand firm and immovable, and work for the Lord always, work without limit, since you know that in the Lord your labour cannot be lost.'

Aunty Betty came to an abrupt stop, and my mother's flapping hand was finally lain to rest.

I caught Nurse Binns saying 'peculiar' and 'out of the ordinary'. My father continued to look calm and disinterested. I would have to be patient about the photograph.

As we wandered over to my mother, Aunty Betty was getting her things together. 'So pleased to have caught you both. Mother's looking so peaceful today. I've been sitting with her for ages.'

She mounted her crutches and leant perilously towards us. 'Mind you, I must say that these nurses are a little taut. Now, I know that they have a difficult job, and Mother can be awkward – but it's not her fault.' She gave my mother a beaming, red, cherubic smile. It seemed as if her cheeks might explode. 'Must go, my dears, Jack will be expecting me in the car park. Goodbye.'

She poled her way unsteadily down the passage, leaving my father and I alone. I looked down at my mother. She looked very poorly indeed. The fight was leaking from her.

By this time, my father had sat down and was patting her hand. There was no doubt that he was distressed. The blood had drained from his dull, waxy face. His tense features suggested he didn't have the capacity to express the feelings which were straining them.

Eventually, I sat down as well, but was unable to touch my mother or speak to my father. We remained silent for twenty minutes or so. Apart from faint, irregular breathing and the occasional blinking of an eyelid, she remained absolutely impassive. Her night-dress had been exchanged for a loose-fitting, paper-based substitute. There were small islands of food on it. Her arm showed bruising where they'd tried to find a vein for the drip, but she was so withered and bony that even the thought of putting a needle in her seemed hideously cruel.

I sensed the cancerous satsuma in her skull, a lumpy fruit.

I remembered how Mother had always insisted on her associations with people who were ill. It was almost if she was deliberately emulating them. Before she had died, Auntie Bernie said of the old lady who had lived in the flat above, 'She's had that heart attack on purpose. Just to prove she's more ill than I am. She can be heartless, you know, that one. She just doesn't know. I'll bloody show her . . .'

Three weeks later, Auntie Bernie was dead.

Now my mother was bloody showing everybody.

Still no words. What on earth is happening? Surely you're not jealous, not after everything we've been through? (William with the Nose has been in contact with Peter Slythe several times. They both pester me. Of course, he fell in love with me, and Jade is out of favour. But so what? Enough is enough.)

Please accept the usual selection of food. I hope that nothing has happened to you. Surely I would have heard something(?) And can't you at least send news of Mama and Papa?

I shall remain calm and still . . . as you once showed me. Nothing out of the ordinary is happening here. More details when I am sure of an audience.

Nr. Stratford. February 4th, 1948.

When we arrived home my father cooked tea in a single orange non-stick saucepan. It was the usual fry-up of eggs, sausages, bacon, beans, bread and mushrooms. The corner shop didn't stock liver. We wiped everything down afterwards, and then he announced that he had to 'go to the office'. I was immediately suspicious. But somehow it didn't seem worth opening up another front. As mother would have said, 'I've got enough on my plate without having to worry about all you buggers as well.'

I watched television and allowed myself a bar of the electric fire. I sat on the floor so as not to disturb the cushions on the sofa. Some things in life were simply too holy. I thought of Aunty Betty: 'They killed the passover lamb on the fourteenth day of the second month: and the priest and the Levites were bitterly ashamed. They hallowed themselves and brought many cushions to the house of the Lord . . .' I knew how those Levites must have felt.

My father hadn't told me what time I should go to bed. A mood of silent, anarchic unaccountability drifted throught the house. The news was on. The miners were still at it. My father called them 'bastards' even though he enjoyed the disruption. President Nixon was causing trouble in the USA. Someone's little girl was safe after all.

I turned the television off.

I went to the outside toilet and uncovered a can of supermarket cola. Then I wandered up to my parents' room. My mother kept a jar of Nivea cream and a book in her bedside table. They were always historical novels. This one had been abandoned a few weeks ago. The front cover featured a well-built negro slave. Behind him was a pretty white girl in a pink dress, running away from a house which was in flames.

Mother's side of the bed smelt of jellied eels.

My father's drawer contained a paperback copy of *Mistresses*. It had been there for a year and a woman with blonde hair smiled up from the cover. I had never worked out whether it was a novel or a kind of handbook. There was also his tiny Russian radio, the size of a matchbox. He liked listening to football results and cricket commentaries in bed. With the earpiece he wouldn't disturb my mother, who invariably retired before him and fell asleep reading with the light on. Lastly, there was a squat, round wooden pot which held cufflinks and shirt stiffeners. This was a relic of my father's proper-shirt-days and a reminder of my mother's reluctance to throw anything away.

It was too early for Christmas presents, so I didn't look in the wardrobe.

I lay back on my bed. The curtains in my room hadn't been closed. Mother always drew them together at the very moment daylight faltered. My routine was inefficient in comparison. I began to stare at a star. There was complete silence. I shut my eyes for a while, then opened them. The star was still there, apparently dislocated from the others around it, in its own space. Independent. It seemed to be looking back. I was watching the star and the star was watching me. There was a sensation of poised balance, of an equal tension. My thoughts poured awkwardly into the suspended moment.

I composed a letter to my mother: 'Dear Mum, I know that you are not very well at the moment and probably don't even understand what I'm saying. Never mind – I'll still carry on, if that's all right. I know about you and Rainer. I read the letters. I found them in Tatters' safe. He and Nanna were the ones who stopped you writing to each other. Did you know that? Maybe this is unwelcome news since you seemed to give up so much when you turned your backs on each other. Why should I complain? After all, if you hadn't married Dad I wouldn't be here. I just wanted you to know that I know and don't mind. And I think you still keep a photograph of Rainer with you in hospital. Even Dad seems to know that one. Please get well soon . . .'

The words evaporated as I heard the telephone ringing. It was Nanna, asking if my father and I would be going round to lunch the next day. I said we would, and she asked whether we'd mind sharing two chops between us, and possibly doing less peas than usual.

Later, as I undressed, I thought about the photograph again. I felt sure about it. Why was such a fuss being made otherwise? But my father hadn't expressed either surprise or shock, almost as if he'd expected it. Maybe he knew about the letters, too. Possibly he was involved in the whole plot. I knew how devious he could be when, as my mother said, 'the mood took him'. If he knew everything, how had he come to accept it? Perhaps it was love, but the thought of my mother and father being in love, falling in love, was just too difficult. He remembered her birthdays at the last moment and she laughed whenever he got his 'doofers' caught in his trouser zip.

I went back to my parents' room and looked in Mother's wardrobe. No presents. There was only a strong smell of mothballs, about thirty leather handbags and a ragged mink stole, its glass eyes fixing me with a vacant stare.

Outside the window, a vast course of time was spreading outwards, staining the dark sky and the rest of the universe, grinding forwards.

. . . I am confused. Are you trying to throw me off the scent? Is there something you are trying to tell me? I wonder if I can't detect Freud's application of the subconscious desire working its way through (?) You know, of course, that I have seen this kind of thing before, in the village, for example (Johannes Steinhalt, for one) – but what use is that to me at the moment?

I am trying to be reasonable. Rational. Calm.

Your letters are short and impatient. They accuse me of not writing. But I am writing. I have to trust that what you are saying is the truth, so I must conclude that nothing seems to be reaching you. But (of course), it follows, you cannot (or will not) even see these words . . . so you will continue to be angry, intolerant.

The whole thing is impossible.

Maybe Mrs Slythe has frightened you away from me. Tell her that I know exactly what she is up to. Tell her from me that as far as you're concerned, the positive lines end on Saturn. Ask her whether the companion line disappears to

the life line. Does the end of the affection line curve upwards?
And is she sure that the event line ends in the area of Saturn
originating in the vicinity of Venus, whilst still smoothly
crossing the life and head lines . . .

   Luneburg. February 1st, 1948.

My curtains were still open when I woke up. I didn't
know what time my father had come home; I must
have been asleep. I noticed a smear on my bedroom
window. I couldn't remember it from the time before
my mother went into hospital.

   The toilet smelt different; maybe we weren't cleaning it the right way. Brown was beginning to appear
around the inside rim of the bath. Greasy, black
fingermarks were smeared over the glossy white
paintwork of almost every door in the house. If I
looked hard into the carpet, I could see small balls of
dirt, fluff and intertwined hair interrupting the flow of
the weave. Unmistakably, strands of hair and grey
carpet fabric were snaking along the skirting boards,
sticking to it. The telephone was now a blur of dull
smudges, the opaque traces of our fingers absolutely
clear. Somehow, we'd worn away patches of the paint
on the walls, leaving them rough, uneven and slightly
darker. Looking back (suddenly) at where I'd been
walking, I could catch the carpet springing apolo-
getically back into place, leaving slight foot-sized
indentations. The bookcase bothered me, too. The
1936 English translation of *Mein Kampf* never seemed
to be flush against the other titles. I wondered whether

I'd put *Black's Medical Dictionary* back properly. Its misalignment could have caused a disturbance. Like snails, we were crawling along, making slime.

My father had done a pile of burnt toast for breakfast. When I put the margarine back into the fridge, my mother's neat shelf patterning and cross-referencing of foods now being in complete disorder, I could only smell something rancid. Islands of waste lay strewn around the individual compartments.

We arrived at Nanna's having said little to each other the whole morning. I was only too glad to get out of the house.

'How is she?' Nanna asked. She could never bring herself to use my mother's name, and clearly wanted to get the whole thing out of the way as quickly as possible.

'Not very well,' my father replied, rather warily.

'I sent some chocolates.'

'Thank you.'

'I don't suppose she'll manage them, though.'

'No. She won't.'

She asked my father to help mash the potatoes, 'to save' her wrists. They had taken a pounding when she'd tried to spread the frozen butter that morning. We sat down to lunch.

After a short while, Nanna said to him, 'I do wish you wouldn't use Biros at the office.'

He used nothing but.

'Why not?'

'They're poisonous.'

'Don't be ridiculous.'

'They are. Get ink from a Biro into your system and you won't think it's funny.'

'I don't think it's funny.'

'No.'

'No.'

'It's easily injected. Just one slip – and the point, the bit the ink comes out of – they're sharp enough to pierce the skin.'

'I can't not use Biros.'

'You be careful then. But don't say I haven't warned you.'

There was a resentful pause before my father continued: 'What's the difference between Biro ink and other ink?'

'Never you mind. There's a difference. That's all you need to know.'

'I use a fountain pen at school,' I added, cheerily.

'Good lad,' said Nanna. 'If only your father was as sensible. I'll just go and warm the ice-cream up.'

I noticed that the chops had been cut completely off the bone and the potatoes pulped into an artless, creamy sludge. The cherries which came with the ripple were ruthlessly un-stoned and limp. Nanna was taking no chances. Even if she wasn't particularly concerned about my mother, the suggestion of illness had affected her. We were all scrutinising our lives carefully.

'Wrap up properly next time you come round,' said Nanna as we were leaving. 'You can never trust summer weather. I won't come to the door. There's a draught. Close it tight behind you. I'll do the chain when you're down the stairs. And drive carefully. Go the long way back. You know what the traffic's like at this time.'

My father drove home fast, the usual way. He wore his hunted expression, chewed the loose skin on his fingers again and played Benny Goodman too loudly.

At school the next morning, it was more convenient to distance myself from my mother's illness. I had moved to the all-boys school with the fighter plane. Every teacher was a man and the day was governed by a bell and the timetable. There simply wasn't room for sentiment, or any kind of deviation from the scrupulously prepared plans of study.

Mark Perkins was also at the school, although in a different class. My mother hadn't minded that my friendship with him had cooled over the years. He had served his purpose.

'He's not growing very fast, is he?' she had said, one day.

'Not particularly,' I cautiously agreed.

'In fact, he's a titch,' she continued. 'Bring some others home if you like.'

I looked apprehensive.

'I'll buy you a bike.'

Initially, she had been worried about 'homos' and 'the kinds of goings-on you get at boys' schools'. But her fears were unfounded, and I eventually got my bike. It was an old BSA model, coloured turquoise and pink. There were no gears or lights. The saddle was stiff and awkward. There was only a small sack attached to the back of the saddle, and that contained a puncture repair outfit. But it was still a bike.

I was beginning to feel very grown-up. One friend had an elder sister who had a record of the *Concert for Bangladesh* and a bra. Another's father owned a butcher's shop and a launderette. But my mother's favourite was the son of the local vicar, who had a goatee beard. She used him as a trump card whenever the going got difficult with Aunty Betty. Mrs Frings' two children had, in her view, 'gone wrong somewhere', so that was another chance to make headway.

'One's a bloody art student,' she said, 'and the other one – the girl – she's married one of those long-haired weirdos and gone into farming. And fruit farming at that. In this country. She wears one of those floppy hats. I think she's a bit funny in the head. But who wouldn't be with a mother like that?'

The teachers at my new school never fell asleep at the board, and they all seemed to possess fierce amounts of energy and brisk efficiency. Mr Bosanko took us for Science; he was very big with wide open blue eyes that were always staring and never seemed to blink. He was particularly good at telling ghost stories and playing guitar during lessons. He also took rugby, which Nanna disapproved of and wanted to have banned. Nanna also wrote to the Headmaster suggesting the use of tennis balls at cricket practice as the usual sort were 'very hard and likely to cause serious injury'. During rugby that day, Mr Bosanko stood in the middle of the field, his legs planted like two enormous oak trees. He invited us all to hurl ourselves at him and try to knock him down. No one succeeded, and he graded the ferocity of our impacts according to the animals we reminded him of. 'Mosquito' or 'fly' were quite common, and occasionally a really large boy would manage 'dog'. Rather exotically, one was a 'llama'. I was 'gerbil'.

We finished rugby early because Mr Bosanko said he had a surprise for us. We were to see something special that we would never forget.

Expectantly, we changed and filed into the Science Laboratory, something of a privilege in itself. We listened attentively whilst he told us that the Fifth Year had been working on reproduction. After a series of teasing questions and tentative answers, Mr Bosanko esablished what it was, exactly, that he would be talking about. Nobody said 'sex', although we were all waiting for it. Someone had told me two years ago that it was all to do with men putting their chimneys into women's holes. My mother said that men weren't to blame – they simply couldn't help it, like going to the toilet. 'That's the way it is,' she'd said. I remembered that a few months ago she'd been especially pleased at the news that three boys had been caned for something that had happened in the changing rooms. 'Quite normal in healthy young boys,' she said accusingly, and placed a box of tissues next to my bed. I looked confused. 'It'll save washing the sheets every time,' she explained.

All this hadn't prepared me for the dead rat. Its four feet were stapled to separate corners of a wooden board. Its front was split open, revealing what Mr

Bosanko called 'the intestinal system and the reproductive organs – a lot of jelly and spaghetti'.

There was a sharp, whistling intake of breath from
the class as he suddenly held the slashed rodent up for
us all to see.

A fat boy called Christopher Pugh fainted.

'Leave him,' said Mr Bosanko. 'I'll give him some
water in a minute.'

The rat was female. The skin from its abdomen had
been cut, folded back and held in place by a row of
three neat, silver tacks on each side of the board. The
skin had a greenish tinge to it. The mouth was slightly
open, and two goofy teeth were showing. The eyes
were only half-closed. Images of my mother lying in
bed at the hospital and of my exploding hamster
came into my mind. There was a kind of awful
symmetry about the thing that was being held up in
front of me.

Mr Bosanko picked up some tweezers and a small
pair of scissors. He explained how everything we
could see worked, and what it was for. For the most
part, I could only hear a damp, rubbery, squelching
noise as he pulled fatty tissues around and probed
ligaments and muscles. There was a dry, brittle sawing
as he finally cut into the rat's reproductive organs to
show more precisely what went on in them.

Tomorrow was the day of my mother's operation.

I wondered whether her head would make the same
easy cracking noise when they sliced it open to get at
the satsuma. They would use a saw. Probably, the
noise would be muffled, dampened by the liquids and
fluids rushing about inside and around her brain.

. . . (i) the cellars, the kitchen and the first floor are complete. Your parents intend to live in these rooms – maybe within the next week or so – and will rent out the second floor. Your father has started to plant a garden, which will stretch all the way down to the brook. Naturally, there are no flowers.

(ii) Your father continues work at the brick factory.

(iii) Heinz plans to open a petrol filling station to supplement his revenue as a blacksmith.

(iv) Hinrichs is still at it – this time, he's after Ingeborg Worlitz. People tolerate him well enough; there's a feeling that we've all been through something more significant than he can offer.

(v) Nati sends a message from Hamburg. She has 'had enough' (her words), and plans to marry a chemist. He is twenty years older than her. Like me, however, she wonders why you have disappeared, and how to make contact.

(vi) The Americans have all but gone from the area. The British stay. There are regular patrols along the Elbe road. There was a great deal of activity on the other side of the river. It appears to have stopped for the moment. I assume the Russians are (therefore) confident of their positions.

(vii) Your father finally got some new teeth. He complains that they are too big for his mouth – but they will do. We all make do, for the present. In such ways, we are reminded that we are not free agents; necessity is still the prevailing law of life. The luxury of choice is almost forgotten. The recognition of necessity keeps a sense of the ridiculous at bay.

(viii) The weather is so cold. The mud stands up in hardened ridges in the fields.

Rainer.
Luneburg. February 12th, 1948.

For Maths homework we had to do Probability, but
my mind wasn't on it. I wondered what would have
happened if my mother had stayed in Germany and
never come to England. Or if Opa had never migrated
from Poland to Hamburg. If Mrs Bacon's ring hadn't
been so uncomfortable, of if my father had visited at a
different time. If he had stayed a little longer here, not
so long there, he could have missed my mother
altogether. Every event in their meeting was charged
with special significance, as if it were somehow
inevitable.

I tried to reduce the circumstances to their simplest
essence. A cup of coffee, for example, which must
have appeared random and arbitrary whilst it was
actually being drunk, now seemed logical, almost
predetermined. At every stage in their lives, my
parents carried with them the residue of previous
experiences. These helped to precondition what was
next. The past waited to slip over the present, like a
glove. Time and time again my mother had almost
predicted the available options until she 'arrived' at
my father. There followed the same recurring question
to which he had become the only feasible answer.
They were both trapped by each other. And my
future, of course, was being shaped at that very
moment. A pattern was forming, even if I couldn't
make it out.

There was a drizzle outside. I walked to the French windows, aware of the carpet behind me playing its tricks. The garden was overgrown, but my mother had never shown my father how to use the lawn-mower, and she wouldn't let him go near the borders. I thought of Aunty Betty's garden and wondered whether Jesus was really in the potting shed.

Even if he wasn't, it might not be a bad idea to have a look, just in case.

Last night, I dreamt that my mother had died. I met her two weeks later living in West Bromwich.

In *Black's Medical Dictionary* I had read that there were several 'Certain Signs of Death', and I examined her for the evidence: 'There are some minor signs, such as relaxation of the facial muscles, which produces the staring eye and gaping mouth of the Hippocratic countenance . . . discoloration of the skin, which becomes of a wax-yellow hue, and loses its pink transparency at the finger-webs.'

'What are you looking at?' she said.

'Nothing,' I lied.

'Yes you bloody well were.'

'Can I see your finger-webs?'

'Please.'

'Please.'

She held a hand up. The left one, I think. The webs looked quite pink to me. Around one of the fingers was a large sapphire ring, set in white gold and

surrounded by a cluster of small diamonds in the shape
of a star.

'Are you sure you're dead?'

'Of course.'

'But what are you doing in West Bromwich?'

'I live here. It could be worse. It might have been
Saltley. You can't just let something like dying bring
everything to a grinding halt. Life goes on. One of
these days you'll learn to appreciate that. You're still
just a nincompoop really.'

Then she said that she'd just been to a 'smashing
new shopping centre' and would I like to come back
to her house for a cup of tea.

'You live in a house?'

'Of course. Don't you?'

I agreed, and on the way there we talked about her
funeral.

'I always wanted to be cremated, you know. Not
buried. That's your bloody father for you. He'd forget
his arse if it wasn't fixed on properly.'

'Wouldn't it hurt – being burnt?'

'Don't be daft. I'm dead.'

The house was small but characteristically neat and
clean. We arrived at 2.35 p.m.

All the clocks inside said 2.50 p.m.

'Old habits die hard,' I said cheerily, gesturing at
the red plastic clock in the kitchen.

'What did you say?'

'Old habits . . .' I started. Then, more airily,
'Nothing.'

The tea-bags were already in their cups, as if my
mother had been waiting for me – or someone.

We drank it down, then she showed me around the house. I noticed how clean everything was; the kettle had been buffed, the taps shined, the rubber plant wiped. Her tea-caddy was almost new, although of the same design as the one back home. I wondered whether there was any tea in this one.

There were no heaters, fires or anything else to heat the house. I saw that the toothpaste had already been squeezed on to her brush ready for the nightly scrub. Along the bristles lay a hardened pellet, a rabbit's dropping gone white.

'I could manage without ceilings or floors, you know,' my mother announced.

'How do you mean?'

'I don't need them. I don't understand all the heebie-jeebie, but apparently . . .' (and here she looked confidential), '. . . I'm in a different dimension. It was all explained, but on the whole I felt I couldn't do without them. I've got used used to them, I suppose. I couldn't change now, not at my age.'

'But you have changed. You're dead.'

'Don't teach your grandmother to suck eggs,' my mother countered. 'Don't you think I don't know that – and worry about it? It's not easy being dead, carrying things around with you all the time; illness, memories. God knows what else.'

'Can't you just start again?'

'You must be joking. Just because you're dead it doesn't mean you can just forget everything. Quite the opposite. You've got a lot to learn.'

It was indisputable. I left promising to call again, but my mother told me that she was busier than ever, especially over the weekend, and to leave it for a few more days when it would be more convenient.

As I walked away from the house, I glanced back and saw that she'd changed into a brown nylon overall with orange trimmings. She climbed up a wooden stepladder and was soon busy polishing the windows with an old pair of knickers.

No letters. No audience. I am losing faith, Rainer. It has been weeks. Is this a test? Has God died again? Don't you dare abandon me, Rainer.

You promised. For ever and ever. Bastard.

Truly, I feel as if I'm living in the arsehole of the world.

Is that wrong?

Nr. Stratford. February 14th, 1948.

My mother's operation was in the afternoon. I lowered myself out of bed, and as I got ready, the day was already taking on a luminous, harsh intensity, as if everything was being subjected to the gaze of a penetrating, steady white light. I thought of Aunty Betty saying that '. . . The light shineth in darkness; and the darkness comprehended it not.' I saw the wallpaper's yellowing, dull-urine edges and the translucent ring-like stains of dried water on the chrome taps in the bathroom. There was a thin layer of dust shimmering on top of the tallboy in my bedroom.

The dark patches around each plastic light switch – themselves a disappointingly nondescript creamy colour – seemed wretched and troublesome. The Sellotape holding the cracked mirror in place on the front of the small bathroom cabinet was orange and peeling at the edges. I went downstairs. If I put my head on a level with the kitchen counter I could see hundreds of salt grains, possibly left over from last night's fry-up; maybe there for even longer. There was also the obscenity of crumbs, scattered around, disturbing the smoothness of the plastic surface. No matter how many times I wiped, there always seemed to be some left. They simply accumulated.

I lay down on the floor and scanned the soft yellow and black line from one end of the kitchen to the other.

It was hopeless.

The floor was covered with dirt, small balls of rolled fatty grease and clusters of fluff. I glanced up – but only slightly. From the new angle, it was possible to see the obscure brown stains that had built-up into an elaborate lacework scale over the bottom of the cupboards.

I rolled over on to my back and stared up at the strip of fluorescent lighting directly above me, illuminating the particles of dust, flaking skin and human fallout that had drifted up into the air directly beneath it.

The world was flowering into unclean matter.

Climbing into the car to drive to the hospital I was oblivious of my father, though aware that his face was detached and serious.

Despite the efforts my mother always made to clean the Mini, the residues of previous journeys still clung to its interior – heelmarks on the rubber mats below the driving pedals; a damp cigarette stub stained with a cheap, pinkish lipstick shade (Olive's?); a network of scratches that covered the seats and the vinyl part of the dashboard, as if two birds had been fighting there. The steering wheel's cleats carried the grease deposited by my father's hands over hundreds of journeys. Part of him was irrevocably smeared around it. There was a small tear on the back seat that gave way to the layers of foamy rubber beneath; I thought it was just big enough to take my mother's tumour. Thinking this brought a satisfying smile to my face.

We drove through the centre of Birmingham, and then headed west for the last few miles towards the hospital she had been transferred to. The rush-hour traffic swept us along in a huge tidal race of gleaming metal and potential accidents.

I didn't notice individual buildings, but gradually I became aware of their accumulated shapes and outlines. The feeling was indistinct but certain, a fleeting visual impression that orginated in the changing forms and heights of each construction, sharpened by the spaces between them.

The road swung around and passed by a group of recently built but already decaying shops. The white wooden paintwork on the front of the 60s parade was peeling, revealing wounds of grey primer. Next to the shops, a neat blood-red Victorian church, much older but in perfect condition. And then, a long grey warehouse, like a ship, built before the Second World War.

These and all the other buildings carried a distinct image of themselves, hundreds of voices proclaiming the times that had elapsed since each had been built. A picture in the mind clarified by the images leaking in through my eyes.

I closed them and felt the dark shapes imprinting themselves. The immense age of the city, the clamour of voices that rose from the buildings and beneath them the ground itself, suggested something vast and deafening. I was carried back through time, reducing everything to meaningless dust and unformed dirt.

We turned into the hospital car park and my father parked. We walked across the tarmac. I could still hear the booming voices around me, and yet each had a separate identity. Each brick, each shovelful of soil, each grain of sand was calling by itself. The sky seemed an infinite babel and I looked up towards the erupting cosmos, resonant with the tuneless words of a time-song. I wondered where the dead centre of this accumulated, massive confusion lay, or whether there was one.

My father broke in. He asked if I could remember which was the way to my mother's ward, and the turbulent medley of tongues I'd been aware of began to fade, and then became silent.

He glanced around to see if Aunty Betty or Mrs Frings were there, and when he couldn't see them, took an indigestion tablet and entered the hospital reception area.

It was about ten-thirty in the morning.

Do you remember when we first met, immediately after your father had returned from Russia? I came upon you in shock, wandering along the road out of the village. You had been crying, but not right then. You were dry and beyond tears. You still looked lovely, and I told you so. I offered you some water, which you took, gulping it down. You wanted to talk. I listened whilst you talked to a stranger about your father.

You told me he had been due back from Russia that day. He had been in a camp for three or four years. You couldn't quite recall. Numbers didn't seem to matter. The bus from Luneburg was due that morning. It was a few minutes late; you didn't mind, but when it arrived and the other passengers had stepped off, your father wasn't on board. You thought there must have been an administrative error. You walked home. What were you feeling? Confused? Numb? Disappointed? You mentioned that your emotions had ceased to function a long time before. When you turned into your kitchen, there was a man, on his knees, licking clean the bowl containing the cat's scraps. This was your father. You had walked straight past him, after all, as he'd got off the bus – face caved in, skin like faded parchment, head bowed low, bones poking through at obscene angles. You hadn't recognised him. He could barely lift his head. His eyes rarely left the ground. His world consisted only in the square metre of space surrounding his feet. You put him to bed. Overcome by what you'd seen, you walked along the road, where I found you.

I was on my way to Hamburg – for work, to continue my studies, or anything I could call 'useful', in fact. I knew immediately I saw you that I must break my journey, and stay. I knew that I must marry you.

214

And we talked. I told you that good things have a habit of declaring themselves in strange ways. Their ambitions are announced crookedly. In order for good to survive, it must accept a pinch of bad – sometimes much more than a pinch. Nietzsche (of course) knew this. For example (I said), his will to life also accepted the need (even) for death. Your father knew what he was doing. It was shameful and humiliating, but it showed he still had the will to life itself within him.

Nietzsche isn't entirely right, though. He also says that evil is man's strength, that in order to become better he also has to become more evil. 'The greatest evil is necessary for the superior man's best . . . I rejoice over great sins as my great consolation'.

We agreed that despite everything, there was no need for evil in order to become better. One could manage perfectly well without the energy, the stimulation, of the other. You understood. In those early days, this was our belief, our faith, our hope. We went from there. You said that it gave you more strength than I could ever realise.

In the following weeks, we talked about the Germany we'd like to help build, the mistakes of the war, about pork dripping and jellied fish.

We argued – about German culture. I told you about my belief in the 'old' Germany, the Aufklärung, when the values of Goethe, Schiller and Brahms impregnated our lives and gave us a rational, enlightened spirit. You agreed, but also wanted to praise jazz music. I was shocked. Even Expressionist Art was dangerous for me; jazz was barbaric. The black musicians . . . I had to admit my prejudices. You persuaded me. You always seemed to push things to their limits. You walked high wires. I adored you.

215

I was not a good lover, but you didn't seem to mind. You said you didn't feel that you had to make me 'feel like a king'. I was the only man you'd ever known for whom this was true.

Out of our differences – but also our similarities – a love was made. I still feel it.

I quoted Freud at you: 'Man must always strive to love, so that he doesn't become sick.'

I am still striving. Maybe this letter will find its mark – by force of will?

At the moment, my life is a series of dreams, played before a solitary audience of one.

My love is no illusion. Act on it. Please.

Always, your beloved Rainer.

Luneburg. February 14th, 1948.

The front of the building looked like a very large bus shelter. A metallic hood shot out from the flat frontage, supported in each corner by a slim metal pole. There was a flight of seven concrete steps up to the shelter, and then an adjoining criss-cross of ramps and walkways, recently added. A ragged mosaic of what looked like enormous bathroom tiles hugged one side of the entrance. It showed a large hand reaching out towards whoever might be entering the hospital and had been accomplished in various shades of bright pink set against an overpowering medicine-bottle blue.

The front doors were wedged open with old green milk crates.

Stray wires blew gently back and forwards in the breeze, suggesting that at some time the entry technology had been more sophisticated. My father looked vaguely disgruntled; he had always had a keen eye for gadgets and no doubt felt cheated that something didn't whir or click on his behalf.

We picked our ways through the foyer and the five or six wheelchairs that had been abandoned there, the occupants looking either anxious or angry. Flickering strips of neon lit up the corridors which webbed out before us, so that the whole effect was eerie and unsettling. Everyone stared, either trying to identify a sick relative or to work out what your ailment could be. It was difficult to differentiate the sick from those who had stumbled in from the outside world. The hospital's peculiar atmosphere brought everybody together. I sensed my warts guiltily trying to re-establish themselves through the skin on my knee. The occasional doctor or nurse who wandered past reminded us all that we were intruders, in one way or another. A 24-hour clock had stuck on 19:48. The walls on both sides exhibited paintings and drawings done by the patients; the one nearest to me showed a man with an arrow through his head. He was haemorrhaging purple blood whilst a red cow in the background chewed the cud. It was signed 'George'.

We walked through the wards, all named after famous battles. My mother was in Waterloo. She'd have been pleased, because some of the battles were really quite minor – little more than skirmishes, in fact. Imagine the fuss if she'd been put in Naseby, for instance. She was a great one for wars and battles, and so the ward had some bearing. 'What we need is a bloody good war,' she'd often said, 'a real purging. I'm sorry, but there are just too many people on earth.'

Everything seemed to be green and there was a faint smell of ammonia mixed with stale pee. Even the flower shop and the mini-bank in the foyer smelt of it. My father had forgotten to buy any flowers.

As we walked through the corridors, each ward took on a particular identity; you could sense it just from peering through their windows.

In one, full of old people, everybody was white and nothing moved. They were like piles of old clothes, somehow starched upright. Death's waiting-room. My mother's ward was at the far end of the East arm, next to a maternity ward called Agincourt. There were about twenty beds, all with tired mothers watching the NHS cots beside them. I felt that I should be feeling at least some curiosity about the miracle of birth, but the only thing I was aware of was a slight spasm of irony at the thought of my mother being in the adjoining room. My father looked uneasy. Maybe he'd made the same connection. Whatever, he took another indigestion tablet. It was round and pale yellow. I used to think they were sweets and ask for 'some'. They had become known as 'somes'. My father was trying to quell the riot in his stomach, to calm his acid gastric juices. His breath smelt, but I didn't say anything. We entered Waterloo.

I could see my mother about halfway down, almost completely surrounded by a green floral-patterned screen. She'd have approved of it, though I doubt she was even aware of its existence. As we closed on her, I could make out a small collection of gifts on her bedside table: Nanna's chocolates, a monstrous pile of dates and some fruit baskets with tags like 'Cheer up – Pete P. and family', 'Our love – Lance and Kath' and 'God Bless – Betty'. My mother was propped up, eyes more or less open but totally unblinking. You could make out every bone in her body. She had definitely shrunk a few inches and her cheeks had simply ceased to exist. Instead, she had a grey hollow on each side of her face. Her head had been completely shaved in preparation for the operation so that it looked outrageously small and vulnerable. You didn't want to even touch the inviting furry black stubble in case her skull cracked. She looked like something from Belsen or Auschwitz. Wrapped around her but falling at strange angles was her old pink dressing-gown.

'The operation is this afternoon,' my father said, taking my mother's hand and looking blankly concerned. I was staring straight ahead. He asked me if I was all right.

My stomach felt as if it was about to burst. Stars and planets, whole galaxies made up entirely of white footballs on a purple background raced over the film of my vision. In less than three hours, somebody was going to put a knife through my mother's head and slice it open.

I didn't think I was too good, but nodded anyway.

My father had brought a copy of the *Daily Telegraph* for her. He put it down, but there was no response.

'I told you she'd prefer the *Mail*.' The joke passed without comment. I felt hot and wanted to do something different. I remembered the photograph that Nurse Binns had mentioned and pretended to puff up and reposition my mother's pillows whilst slipping my hand underneath them to search for it. There was nothing there, or on the bedside table. Either that, or it was buried underneath the mountain of bruised, useless fruit. A nurse approached round the side of the screens and said, 'The operation's at one-thirty. It will be long, but we don't know how long. It depends on how stubborn the tumour is.' We also learned that:

(a) my mother hadn't been to the toilet for three days;

(b) my mother was so weak that even a drip didn't work any more;

(c) there was the possibility that my mother might have an ear infection.

After she'd finished, the nurse smiled mechanically, inverted the watch on her blouse, tapped it smartly a few times and moved off.

My father bought me lunch in the hospital canteen, and I had a runny egg and chips. We talked about football.

'The attack's fine, but the midfield never wins the ball. The defence needs a lot of work – a strong central defender would probably do for now.'

'I suppose the idea is that if they attack a lot, then it doesn't matter so much about the rest.'

'But people like Campbell are passengers for a lot of the games.'

'Especially the away games.'

'Especially the away games.'

'A nice footballer – but he just doesn't get stuck in.'

'George Smith's all right, though.'

'He's got a big nose – but he's all right.'

'I've worked it out, looking at all the games left to the end of the season, that they're bound to get more points than Millwall.'

'How many more?'

'It's close – 54 to 52 – but I think that's expecting the worst. The one I'm unsure about is Cardiff. I've put us down for a win – but they're having a good spell at the moment.'

'What about the Portsmouth game?'

'A win – but you could be right. Maybe I should do it as a draw. Surely they won't lose that one, though?'

'*If* they get promoted – and I say *if*: it's all too close to say at the moment – we must get tickets for next season.'

For dessert I had ice-cream and hot custard. Then my father went to the office, leaving me with the fare to catch the number 37 home.

Dear Herr Welt,

You do not know me, or at least we have not met, but I suspect you know a little of my son.

Whatever, I have to tell you that he has been seeing a Miss Buhl, and has formed something of an attachment to her. My wife and I are not disagreeable to the association. She seems a nice girl, and my son seems very 'struck' on her. That is good enough for us.

We felt that this was the most apposite time to

221

communicate with you, as there are increasingly
hopeful signs that, given the correct
circumstances, their liaison could bear fruit.

You will, I'm sure, appreciate my concern for
our son's future happiness. Naturally enough,
my wife considers it something of a priority,
especially since the war years made it difficult for
him to make any progress in this area. One day,
you may well become a parent yourself; then, I
am certain you will see the wisdom in our
behaviour.

Let us just say that it has come to my notice
that you also have an association with Miss Buhl
– most recently manifested in a number of letters
that you have sent to her.

I ought to inform you that since this became
apparent, I have taken active steps to prohibit the
continued receipt of these letters by Miss Buhl.
She in her turn, of course, knows nothing of this
arrangement.

How this has been accomplished need not
concern you, although I should like to say that
this action in no way implies a personal
judgment upon your character. On the contrary,
your persistence in this matter does you credit.

The reason that I have taken such trouble to
inform you of the situation is that my wife and I
wish my son to be able to pursue his aspirations
without the hindrance your continued writing
would inevitably present.

I hope you appreciate the position we find
ourselves in, and will respect it in the same way

222

that we have come to sympathise with your own predicament. However, and it barely needs saying, you must be assured that no letters from you will ever reach Miss Buhl, and that for the forseeable future, as far as she is concerned, you will cease to exist.

It is also worth mentioning that any attempts to visit England have already been dealt with. The present political climate is useful in this respect, but do not despair – I am sure that foreign travel will reappear on your agenda at some time.

Meanwhile, please accept my best wishes, and remember, 'There are plenty more fish in the sea!' as we say.

Yours respectfully . . .

Birmingham. February 14th, 1948.

It was about two-thirty when I arrived, but I didn't go straight home. Instead, I headed towards the shops in the centre of town. The bus driver had been looking at me in a peculiar way, but I thought, 'I bet your mother doesn't have a brain tumour', and that made me feel better. I had about an hour before school finished, and people I knew came through the shopping square on their way home. My father had written a note explaining the situation and why I should have the day off, and I didn't want anybody to see me – mainly because the washing was piling up at home and I was wearing my last pair of clean trousers – a pair of turquoise cords, fashionable about three years ago and now too small. The shirt wasn't very convincing, either; dark brown cotton with a round-edged bunny collar and two exuberant splashes of light brown ('fawn') on the shoulders – a kind of mock-cowboy piece. I didn't look good.

I walked into W. H. Smiths and went to the book section, even though I didn't much care for books. *Beau Geste* had been a disaster and I couldn't remember much else since *One Hundred and One Dalmatians* several years earlier. I took a book by somebody called John Steinbeck, *The Red Pony*, and idled out of the shop. Nobody stopped me, so I thought I'd try the same thing at a chemist's shop, which also stocked a few records. I didn't care for Bob Dylan, either, but took one of his albums anyway, and stored it under my arm. It was called *Bringing It All Back Home*, and would have cost me £2.39.

In the next forty-five minutes I took four Mars bars, a packet of cigarettes, two pairs of underpants, another book (on yoga, as far as I can remember) and three packs of chewing-gum. The trick was always to look as though you weren't stealing anything, as people would only challenge you if you issued an invitation; if you tried to hide things up your sleeve or under a jacket, that might have acted as a prompt. I stopped when I was almost seen taking a tie (rusty brown with thin red bars, slanting diagonally), though I blamed myself for drawing attention to the procedure by looking cautiously around beforehand and taking too long over handling it. (Note: always check the shop windows, as I read somewhere that store detectives usually operate outside the stores and look *in* on shoplifters.)

I walked home past the hospital with the steaming pipes (which were fizzing like a coffee percolator that day) and dumped everything except the chewing-gum and a pair of underpants in a litter bin.

At home, I ate the chewing-gum – remembering Nanna and taking great care not to swallow any – and drank a can of cola from the outside toilet. I noted that we were down to the last five cans. I switched on the television. We'd only just got colour, and I still regarded this as something of a humiliation. Ten years ago, we were the first in the road to receive BBC2, but we were lagging behind everybody else by at least eighteen months in colour reception. There was a programme on about clever pets and I watched a chihuahua peeling and eating a banana.

Afterwards, I went upstairs and searched through my parents' bedroom. There was nothing new, but I took my turquoise cords and underpants off and tried on a pair of my mother's tights, something I'd always wondered about. They were American Tan in colour and on the small size, but the effect wasn't unpleasant. I walked around in them for a few minutes and even checked myself in the bathroom mirror, having to balance on the lip of the bath itself as all the mirrors were at head height. Then they began to itch and I felt myself self-consciously sweating beneath the fine mesh, so I rolled the tights back down my legs, got dressed, and then threw them into the dustbin at the side of the house.

In the evening, I found myself in my parents'

bedroom again, looking through their window at a girl with short blonde hair taking a dog for a walk on the strip of green grass running parallel with our road. She was still in her school uniform (minus the tie); a dark purple blazer, pale purple shirt and a dark skirt (maybe even black – certainly a very dark blue) and – I noticed – black tights. The dog was a labrador and rather overweight; as it lolloped along, I could see ripples of fat rolling up and down its creamy body. I passed the time by inventing ways to talk to this girl, whom I called Anna. My favourite method was to kidnap the dog and lock him in our garage, and then run out to her all concerned when she was looking for him and say that I'd help her. We'd split up to conduct the search, and then (after a suitably anxious period of time), I'd emerge with Danny (or Rex or whatever he was called, but eventually I decided on Danny) and present him to Anna. We'd get talking and she'd be very grateful for my gallantry and accept an invitation to see *Diamonds are Forever*, which was showing at the local cinema.

Just before I went to bed, the telephone rang and someone asked for my father. I said that he wasn't at home yet, but that I'd be delighted to take a message. It was a woman speaking in an Irish accent. She sounded very angry and said, 'You can tell your father not to come round here bothering us and knocking on my door at all hours of the night. As far as I am concerned, we had an arrangement to go down to Devon this weekend, and I don't want to hear his excuses. Now – will you tell him that?'

I said that I'd try, and as I was replacing the receiver

the phone rang again. This time it was my father with news of my mother's operation.

'She was in there for five and half hours. The tumour's out. She's asleep. We can go and look at her tomorrow. But no talking. The doctors seem pleased. Now it's a matter of waiting.'

I told him about the other call and he wondered 'what on earth it could be about'.

Before going to bed, I trod on his Russian radio and finished the last stick of chewing-gum.

It was about ten-thirty.

Be certain that I shall use every device at my disposal to arrive in England as soon as it is humanly possible. You are what we call in Germany KAKERLATSCHE.

At least tell me how she is.

Luneburg. February 20th, 1948.

— 3 —

The operation was over and my mother wasn't dead. The phrase they used was 'very poorly'. The weekend was looming and I took the next few days off school; my father was sure they would understand. He visited my mother every day, taking in things she was able to ask for, including soap and Nivea face cream. She couldn't move, she'd lost four stones in weight, and I didn't go to see her.

Instead, I went to the cinema and saw (by myself) a double-bill of *Diamonds are Forever* and *From Russia With Love*. At other times, I stayed at home or went to the shops. I found an old raincoat that had belonged to Tatters. He had been a small, rotund man but it fitted me well enough and was also baggy under the arms. I quickly learned how to take and conceal objects, practicing at home with *Mein Kampf*, my mother's potboilers, and the *Illustrated History of the Second World War* in royal-blue hardback covers and in a series of five bulky volumes.

My first visit established a system. I would walk slowly around a shop, carefully checking on faces and postures, working out which ones belonged to any store detectives. Then I would select an object – usually in an unpopulated corner of the shop, which would limit choice, but then it wasn't as if I was actually choosing things that I needed – and somehow or other get it under the raincoat. There were four particular methods I favoured:

(a) Slipping the object in as quickly as possible in the hope that nobody would see me; this usually involved a preliminary glancing check and was the most audacious and straightforward procedure.

(b) Picking two objects up, and then in the act of putting one back, simultaneously slipping the other into the coat and rapidly clenching it under the arm. The idea here was that anybody watching would be satisfied by the more obvious movement of replacing the first object. This worked particularly well with books.

(c) Kneeling down and inspecting something, but at the same time masking my movements with the coat and picking an object up whilst nobody could be certain what was happening. Speed and an innocent appearance were vital here.

(d) Simply picking something up and walking out of the shop with it. Then, because the offence was so blatant, I could always claim that I'd just forgotten about the article, having only picked it up for inspection.

I decided to collect Bob Dylan albums, and in only a few days, managed *John Wesley Harding*, *Nashville Skyline*, *The Greatest Hits* (Volumes One *and* Two), and the soundtrack to *Pat Garrett and Billy the Kid*. In addition, I took 15 KitKats, 12 Mars bars, 16 packets of Treets, 5 Bounties (plain chocolate), 7 Turkish Delights, 4 packets of razor blades, 4 more John Steinbeck novels (including one which I actually read, *Of Mice and Men*), five other books (including a thick yellow copy of *Wisden: The Cricketers' Almanack*, which was difficult to keep wedged under my arm – in the end I had to feign an arm injury and hold it at a strange angle to stop it from dropping to the floor), a small pair of kitchen scales, 16 rubber suction pads (assorted colours) to hang kitchen towels on, 2 pairs of seashell earrings, a pair of replacement American Tan tights, some batteries, a magazine on motor-racing, 3 bottles of cough mixture and a packet of cigarettes (which, out of respect for my mother, I didn't smoke).

I wanted cleaning fluids, but the bottles were the wrong shapes – especially designed to seem awkward and indestructible. There was no chance of slipping one of them under an arm or up a sleeve. Instead, the kitchen scales, which folded flat in a convenient-sized box, would have to do.

But, most of the time, I stayed in the house. For three (or maybe four) days I only went to shop. If my father came home, it was only late at night; every morning there would be a five-pound note on what my mother called the kitchenette, wedged underneath his waffle maker, which was next to the ice-cream maker and the soda-siphon.

I tidied the house, wrote a diary and began to pray.

I packaged all my football programmes up and piled

them in reverse chronological order of matches played.

To regulate time, and to keep everything consistent with the red plastic clock in the kitchen, I moved all the other clocks forward by fifteen minutes.

At the same times every day, I telephoned the hospital: at 11 a.m. (after the dusting), at 2 p.m. (after lunch and Hoovering) and at 4.30 p.m. (after writing my diary and if I'd been out to the shops).

The answer was always the same – that my mother was doing as well as could be expected in the circumstances. I would listen to the disinterested voice processing the information whilst sipping a can of cola.

My father never insisted that I went to see her. And I was glad that he wasn't in the house.

On the fifth day, I spent my father's money on some flowers and visited Aunty Betty.

'Keep far our foes, give peace at home/Where thou art guide, no ill can come,' she breathed into the microphone, and then played it back just to make sure I'd heard.

I said that I'd been praying, and she said, 'That's nice. Are those chrysanthemums? They look lovely. Jack will put them in a vase later on. How's mother?'

'She'd doing as well as could be expected . . .'

'Yes, of course she is,' flashing perfect white teeth in a necklace of a smile – the only part of her that was still whole and uncontaminated if my mother was to be believed. 'Poor soul.'

She was lying in bed surrounded by bottles of medicine and a box of pale-green paper tissues. There was no smell at all.

'Have you been to see her yet?'

'No. But I do pray.'

'A wise man maketh a glad father: but a foolish son is the heaviness of his mother,' she said.

'How's your porphyria?' I asked.

'Never mind my porphyria. When are you going to visit your mother in hospital?'

I stared at the hot-water bottle, lying cold, flaccid and redundant on top of the floral bedspread.

There was a long silence; I heard clocks ticking. I wondered why I was sitting next to this diseased woman who kept God at the bottom of the garden. I had only visited her because it was what my mother would have wanted. Aunty Betty was ruining the plan.

'I'll go tomorrow,' I said.

'Saturday?'

'Yes.'

'Now, you'll really go, my dear?'

'Yes.' I felt helpless when she called me 'dear'.

'A joyful and pleasant thing it is to be thankful,' she smiled. 'Be a poppet and pass the mints.'

I reached over to the dresser, passed the mints and said goodbye. Aunty Betty was smiling, her head turning slowly from one side to the other like a ventriloquist's dummy.

On the way out, I went through the kitchen and took a clothes brush and a box of Nesquick (brown, chocolate). I slid them easily under my arm and walked home trying to whistle Ellington's 'The Dicty Glide'.

One final chance, Rainer – for old time's sake. A fat chance, too, I shouldn't wonder.

I told you this would happen, that you'd abandon me, that you'd end up like the rest. 'The rest?' you asked, all innocent – don't give me that!

Out of habit, I am still writing. 'A woman should always write to her lover.' Recognise that? Don't count on it much longer.

I even tried to think of you yesterday, or was it the day before? I went to my bedroom, as I used to, and lay on my back, motionless, staring at the plaster flaking off the wall. It was dark, a dirty green. A small spider crawled along the ceiling. I collected my thoughts and remembered . . . I'd have given everything, you know . . . why did you involve me? Did you have to? A bet? A joke? No; you told me that you loved me. I believed in you. You led me on. I can still feel you . . . but now the gilt really is coming off on my hands.

You know, I've never felt such high regard for myself together with such contempt for everybody else.

Nr. Stratford. March 19th, 1948.

I arrived back home and made myself supper (a fry-up; two sausages, fried egg, baked beans and three slices of toast – white). I went upstairs, invented a new prayer, organised my record collection alphabetically (from the Allman Brothers to Yes; jazz formed a separate category and Holst's *Planets* was left at the end, on its own) and poured half a bottle of bleach into the toilet. Then I dusted and tidied my mother's

233

wardrobe for the second time that day. I squeezed a pellet of toothpaste on to my toothbrush ready for the nightly scrub before I went to bed. That would be in about four hours. I went downstairs, switched on the television, and watched *Psycho*. It had said in that morning's *Daily Mail*, 'Surely no introduction is needed for Hitchcock's best film . . .'

It took a long time to become gruesome – and then not frighteningly so. And it was, of course, only in black and white. One line made me laugh: 'Mother's not quite herself today.' I worried about the black blood in the bathroom after the shower murder. The mess was cleaned up too easily. What happened to the mop? (Surely, I reasoned, better to use toilet paper and flush the evidence away.) The woman's eye was still and stared up on the other side of the screen. I wondered who was buried in Mrs Bates' coffin if her bones were still sitting in a rocking chair. There was something comic about being slaughtered by a madman in a cheap wig.

To prove I wasn't scared, I went to the outside toilet for the last can of cola, and didn't even turn the garage light on. I also ran a bath. Now I could have one whenever I wanted, though I was still careful to replace the plug in its correct hiding place afterwards, when the last drop of water had been whirlpooled away.

The telephone rang at 10.37 p.m.

My father asked me if I was coming to the hospital the next day. He said that my mother was getting stronger, though she was still very fragile.

I said, 'Yes, if you like.'

There was a pause whilst he inhaled deeply and noisily. His polyps were still a problem.

'I'll pick you up at eleven. I'll be working late tonight.'

Before going to bed I looked in *Black's Medical Dictionary*; my father had a small tumour of mucous membrane in his nose. But he seemed fine.

I don't know if this will reach you, Rainer, and I'm not sure that I care any longer. Your silence is dreadful. At first I was worried but my enquiries found that you and Mama and Papa were all well. Men are all the same. This sort of thing always happens in the end. You're no different.

Our situation doesn't bear much looking into, Rainer – it would only make things more difficult. The past fucks you up. Now I need to overcome it; we need some of that famous inability to feel guilt or remorse which we Germans are supposed to have, our very own VERGANGENHEITSBEWÄLTIGUNG.

I feel calm. I've been seeing the jeweller. He is easy and safe. He wants to look after me. Poor sod – maybe I will let him. What was it Dulcie Slythe said? Anyway, I am about to make my wonderful choice. Do you want to change my mind? Do you think I'd let you?

Remember you telling me that sexual drive evades the responsibility of love, and that love is a kind of prison? Well I'm sick to the back teeth with the responsibility, even if I've been left with about as much desire as one of Papa's bricks.

And how about old Nietzsche and that 'flying into the ideal' when trouble arrives? Not me – I've got no yellow streak – I'll show courage in the face of the reality you've left me with. Germany came off the rails because of its idealism, and now we all have to ask forgiveness. I forgive you too, Rainer – but don't ask for anything more. That's it. You'll be pissing into the wind if you do.

Maybe that's what I'm doing at the moment. I wonder if you're out there? It was you who told me that we all need illusions in order to act. And Dulcie Slythe's are as good as anybody else's. We're all searching for New Heavens after the last few years. Mine are very humble, Rainer, and I shall start by working for J. Arthur Rank in Stratford. He is my limit for the moment. And anyway, movies have such good stories. I'll get to see them all free.

Even if you have a mind to, there's no need to worry. But neither will I lose sleep if you do. It's really all the same to me.

Nr Stratford. April 26th, 1948.

– 4 –

My father picked me up in the morning. As far as I can remember, he was about fifteen minutes late. We didn't speak and 'Dimuendo and Crescendo in Blue' was playing on the car stereo. We passed the Ox and Sun pub. There was another fag-end in the ashtray, plus a small pyramid of tobacco fallout. I registered the fact; my father didn't smoke. He didn't even eat sprouts. I saw a cat hit by a cream and blue bus; it jumped around energetically before gradually laying itself to rest.

We walked past the cartoon hand at the entrance to the hospital and made our way to my mother's ward. The Waterloo Ward. For the first time I noticed how the wards were organised; a series of bays, four beds to a bay and about six bays per ward. I saw that all the walls were painted in different colours, mostly variations of orange, brown, lime green and yellow. There had also been an attempt to match the lino. But it was still a hospital. There was no escaping that.

A young doctor ambled by with a Mickey Mouse badge pinned to his white coat.

We went past Trafalgar. Voices drifted out to the corridor.

'Has Hilary been telling you about her friends?'

'Yes, dear . . .'

I didn't particularly want to see my mother. Or rather, I didn't particularly not want to see her, either. I didn't think particularly of her at all.

I wondered what she'd think if I told her I knew where she'd hidden the plugs and fuses.

We entered her ward. On our right was an elderly woman, sponging herself down in bed. There was no flesh on her, but what there was still sagged as if gravity were fighting her bones for possession of it. On the left stood a battered lime-coloured enamel trolley with a kidney-shaped dish containing what looked like a set of stainless-steel pliers and a long strip of disposable hypodermic needles sneaking out of a green and white box.

I divided all the patients into four main groups: Sure To Die, On the Sickly Side, Messily Ill, and Mad. My mother, I was sure, spilled into at least three of them.

When we reached her bed (still behind the floral screens), I noticed a catheter tube which led to the plastic bag hanging limply on a metallic stand. It was part-filled with a translucent, pale-daffodil-coloured liquid and a puffy cloud of sediment. Her face was sunken, full of dark valleys, her eyes enormous and staring straight ahead. She wore a blue dishcloth over her head.

'She wanted it,' my father said, the first words since we'd entered the hospital. 'To hide the scars. I brought it from the office.'

It did nothing of the sort. A crucifix of centipedes angrily ridged her skull, rising crimson above the soft black down that was just beginning to grow again.

She tried to smile, but only pain showed, and I saw goose-bumps forming on her turkey-skin arms. I knew she'd understand why I hadn't been to visit. We all do what we can; what we have to. Rainer knew that. 'That's the way it is.'

'Don't stand there all akimbo,' she croaked, closing her eyes. The low rasp severed the air.

I bent down and kissed her lightly on the cheek. It was moist from the Nivea cream and smelt of rose water.

As my head bobbed up again, I caught sight of the mysterious photograph. It was propped up on the bedside table against a jug of opaque water, next to a new box of After Eights from Nanna. It was curled at the edges and veined with creases. Black and white. A man holding a newspaper and sitting on a concrete step. He was smiling and wore an open-necked shirt with the sleeves rolled up, revealing thin, quite hairless arms. He looked strange out of uniform, but it was without doubt Adolf Hitler. Adolf Hitler smiling.

My mother caught the moment and spoke. 'I looked at him. My God – it was like a voice calling to me from deep inside a well. Calling me, time and time again. Calling me and pulling me up. He was there, all the time . . .'

My father's lips went thin, though he still held her hand. The colour had gone absolutely from his face.

But I knew what she meant, and didn't reproach her. You couldn't always do what people expected.

She appreciated that and, at that moment, understood me.

She went on, slow and grinding. 'See that woman over there. She's had Reduction Mammoplasty. Her tits were too big, so they sliced a bit off and drained them.' She was trying not to laugh; it would have been too painful. 'Then they cut the nipples to size and sewed them back on. They didn't do such a good job. Every time she stretches, her nipples shoot round the back of her arms. And that old fatty over there. She drank some Ajax. They used a bit of intestine to replace the windpipe. You can hear her farting through her mouth. I'm not badly off, really. You know, my first feeling when I smelled the air was one of gratitude. I'm all right, I thought. Time – is starting all over again . . .'

It was now 12.15 p.m.

I looked at my father and wondered whether it was all right to open the marzipan.

. . . *I had a friend. A nice boy – you would have thought so. He was only seventeen – same age as me – and was called up in the last weeks of the war. He didn't want to fight. The uniform was too big – it used to be someone else's and made his arse look baggy. And it wasn't really. There was a bullet hole in the chest pocket. But nobody really expected him to fight. Even the officers knew it was all up. Then the Russians came. Just our luck – the Americans couldn't get their pontoon bridge ready on time.*

The first ranks trickled into the village. Many were

drunk, some were nearly naked. An overpowering smell of sweat and shit came from them. Some had even thrown their weapons away. Probably they had also got fed up with the whole thing.

This first lot came in a group, down the main road that leads to the Elbe. They were causing some damage – not much – to windows, buildings, what was left of the gardens. They didn't appear to be more than a little curious, teasing rather than aggressive. Then they saw Rolf's uniform. There were no other soldiers, and Rolf didn't think of himself as one. He made himself scarce in a wrecked bus, but the Russians were onto it, rocking it from side to side and shouting, and banging their fists on the body. One of them fired a shot in the air. The rest of us dared not move. A stone hit and shattered the windscreen.

'Tell them I'm not really a soldier. For God's sake, tell them.' I remember Rolf's voice. It was high.

In a minute, the bus was turned over.

Rolf was strong and tall – it took the Russians several minutes to pull him through the jagged windscreen. His face, his hands, his ankles, were all bleeding.

The soldiers tossed him from one group to the next. One of them threw a grenade, and the bus burst into flames. Still, we watched.

I could see the fear on Rolf's face. He was dropped and kicked several times before being hoisted high again. Then, he stopped struggling – his left arm was pulled from its socket, and the pain must have driven him into unconsciousness.

I followed the Russians down the street. When Rolf came to, he was being carried and bounced along the pitted road. There was a brief hold-up and he called for help. Someone shot his right hand away. A few yards further on, they heaved him into the Elbe. He bobbed to the surface and was hit on the temple by a small rock that fizzed at him through the air. One of the soldiers told his friends to stop. He waded in and pulled Rolf out by the collar. He was barely alive. The soldier drew a revolver and shot Rolf through the head. Then he was thrown into the Elbe again, which sucked him down and pulled him under. Then he was gone.

I simply stopped believing.

Eights months later, I met you. Now it's done. Begun and ended.

Nr. Stratford. May 15th, 1948.

You are right. I have no love left in me. How could anything remain of a sentiment that has been so shamefully betrayed. Could not so simple a heart (simple, not sweet or soft?) have accepted good as easily as it was swallowed by greed and selfish indifference?

My philosophical note: it is strange how many circumstances, unconnected with ourselves, appear to maintain the frightening balance between decency and corruption in our hearts.

You will not see me again. I shall leave for . . . well, that is no business of yours. But wherever, I shall forget what has happened, as far as I am able. I shall certainly try to forget you, whose memory could only inflame my soul, when it would be better left as dead.

Luneburg. September 8th, 1948.

LOUIS DE BERNIÈRES

Captain Corelli's Mandolin

In war-torn Cephallonia a young Italian, Captain Antonio
Corelli, is left in charge of the occupying troops. At first he
is ostracised by the locals, but as a conscientious but far from
fanatical soldier, whose main aim is to have a peaceful war,
he proves in time to be civilised, humorous – and a
consummate musician.

When the local Doctor's daughter's letters to her fiancé –
and members of the underground – go unanswered, the
working of the eternal triangle seems inevitable. But can this
fragile love survive as a war of bestial savagery gets closer and
the lines are drawn between invader and defender?

'*Captain Corelli's Mandolin* is an emotional, funny, stunning
novel which swings with wide smoothness between joy and
bleakness, personal lives and history . . . it's lyrical and angry,
satirical and earnest'

Observer

Louis de Bernières is in the direct line that runs through
Dickens and Evelyn Waugh . . . he has only to look into his
world, one senses, for it to rush into reality, colours and
touch and taste'

A. S. Byatt, *Evening Standard*

'*Captain Corelli's Mandolin* is a wonderful, hypnotic novel of
fabulous scope and tremendous iridescent charm – and you
can quote me'

Joseph Heller

'A true diamond of a novel, glinting with comedy and
tragedy'

Daily Mail

GORDON BURN

Alma Cogan

'Gordon Burn takes Britain's biggest selling vocalist of the 1950s, and turns her story into an equation of murder and celebrity. It is a work of extraordinary daring . . . an amazing feat'

The Times

'Burn's bizarre, brilliant novel . . . explores the murky side of fame; the menace and corruption lurking in the wings . . . An extraordinary novel that claws at the imagination. It is the fictional equivalent of a Sylvia Plath poem, not quite understood but impossible to get out of your head'

Daily Mail

'Heaping praise on this magnificent book leads you into cliché – whole passages from it go on buzzing inside your head after you've finished it. A stunning debut'

Sunday Times

'This astonishing novel – abundant, engrossing, imaginatively punchy . . . a sort of *Tristram Shandy* of the entertainment business . . . In its engagement with the modern demonic, it has the kick of a mule – or of Martin Amis at his doomy best'

Times Literary Supplement

'A piece of fiction that is, quite literally, in a class of its own . . . brilliantly inventive, brilliantly realised'

Time Out

LESLEY GLAISTER

TRICK OR TREAT

'*Honour Thy Father* by Lesley Glaister was one of last year's treats, a first novel with an unmistakable voice, it won the Somerset Maugham Prize and one of the Betty Trask awards. *Trick or Treat*, her second, is even better . . . Three adjoining houses in a northern town. In one, huge Olive and puny Arthur, 17 and 7 stone respectively, still adoring after 50 years of happy, left-wing, free love, their anti-fascist posters still drooping from the walls . . . In the next, pregnant Petra and her brood . . . and in the next Nell with her mad search for cleanliness and her dirty, middle-aged son, a child-molester . . . Here are lives of dreadful messiness somehow, through love, achieving grace'

Isabel Quigley, *Financial Times*

'As black as molasses, and, in an odd sort of way, as sweet . . . The author has a glorious, flesh-creeping talent for the macabre'

Kate Saunders, *Cosmopolitan*

'Gamey, fetid, squalid old age is a condition that Lesley Glaister writes about with delicate relish . . . Her writing is extraordinary; her tales of scarcely imaginable horror jumbled up with everyday comforts produce an Ortonesque effect that gives rise to shivery laughter '

Penny Perrick, *Sunday Times*

JAMES KELMAN

HOW LATE IT WAS, HOW LATE

Winner of the 1994 Booker Prize

Sammy's had a bad week – most of it's just a blank space in his mind, and the bits that he can remember, he'd rather not. His wallet's gone, along with his new shoes; he's been arrested then beaten up by the police and thrown out on the street – and he's gone blind.

He remembers a row with his girlfriend, but she seems to have disappeared; and he might have been trying to fix a bit of business up with an old mate, but he's not too sure. Things aren't looking too good for Sammy, and his problems have hardly begun.

'Forging a wholly distinctive style from the bruised cadences of demotic Glaswegian, Kelman renders the hidden depths of ordinary lives in sardonic, abrasive prose which is more revealing of feelings than could ever be expected . . . as uplifting a novel as one could ever hope to read'
Sunday Telegraph

'*How late it was, how late* is gritty, realistic and bleak, but the overall tone is strangely positive. The fast pace of the narrative, Kelman's dry humour and . . . indomitable spirit combine to provide a liberating read'
Big Issue

'Beautiful, spirited thoughts hard up against the old brute truths . . . enormous artistic and social depth . . . James Kelman's best book yet'
Guardian

'A passionate, scintillating, brilliant song of a book'
Independent

NICHOLAS MOSLEY

Hopeful Monsters

'Quite simply, the best English novel to have been written
since the Second World War'

A. N. Wilson, *Evening Standard*

'This is a major novel by any standard of measurement. Its
ambition is lofty, its intelligence startling, and its sympathy
profound. It is frequently funny, sometimes painful,
sometimes moving. It asks fundamental questions about the
nature of experience . . . It is a novel which makes the greater
part of contemporary fiction seem pygmy in comparison'

Allan Massie, *The Scotsman*

'A gigantic achievement that glows and grows long after it is
put aside'

Jennifer Potter, *Independent on Sunday*

'Enormously ambitious and continuously fascinating . . .
There is an intellectual engagement here, a devouring deter-
mination to investigate, to refrain from judgement while
never abandoning moral conventions, that is rare among
British novelists – for that matter, among novelists of any
nationality'

Paul Binding, *New Statesman and Society*

'Nicholas Mosley, in a country never generous to experi-
mental writing, is one of the more significant instances we
have that it can still, brilliantly, be done'

Malcolm Bradbury

'An expansive and liberating adventure of tests, quests,
miracles and coincidences . . . It stands as a well-weathered,
very benign, widespreading kind of tree, drawing sustenance
from the dark earth of a 20th-century experience, and
allowing all kinds of unexpected illuminations to shine
through'

Michael Ratcliffe, *Observer*

SUE TOWNSEND

REBUILDING COVENTRY

'Sue Townsend is just irresistibly funny, and in Coventry she has found the perfect character through which to express not only her humorous view of the human condition, but also her cut-the-shit perceptions of contemporary Britain . . . Everything in *Rebuilding Coventry* is done with ruthlessly satisfying economy. This is satire in the best, Jonsonian tradition, with nothing and no one spared'

New Statesman and Society

'The dialogue is splendidly witty and accurate, and the social observations sharp and imaginative. And the black, comical ending is typical Townsend'

Sunday Express

'Nasty, naughty, funny, brash. I found this swift novel a racy delight'

Joseph Heller

'*Rebuilding Coventry* has the beautiful and unique quality of the folktale, almost as if it had been translated from some exotic and mysterious culture, with the disquieting magic and haunting dream-logic of classic parable. Truly delightful'

Terry Southern

'Wonderfully funny and as sharp as knives'

Sunday Times

A Selected List of Fiction Available from Minerva

While every effort is made to keep prices low, it is sometimes necessary to increase prices at short notice. Mandarin Paperbacks reserves the right to show new retail prices on covers which may differ from those previously advertised in the text or elsewhere.

The prices shown below were correct at the time of going to press.

☐ 7493 9754 3	**Captain Corelli's Mandolin**	Louis de Bernières	£6.99
☐ 7493 9962 7	**Senor Vivo and the Coca Lord**	Louis de Bernières	£5.99
☐ 7493 9857 4	**The Troublesome Offspring of Cardinal Guzman**		
		Louis de Bernières	£6.99
☐ 7493 9130 8	**The War of Don Emmanuel's Nether Parts**	Louis de Bernières	£4.99
☐ 7493 9816 7	**Alma Cogan**	Gordon Burn	£5.99
☐ 7493 9124 3	**Honour Thy Father**	Lesley Glaister	£4.99
☐ 7493 9960 0	**Trick or Treat**	Lesley Glaister	£4.99
☐ 7493 9883 3	**How late it was, how late**	James Kelman	£6.99
☐ 7493 9112 X	**Hopeful Monsters**	Nicholas Mosley	£7.99
☐ 7493 9618 0	**Shear**	Tim Parks	£5.99
☐ 7493 9704 7	**Ulverton**	Adam Thorpe	£5.99
☐ 7493 9747 0	**Swing Hammer Swing!**	Jeff Torrington	£5.99
☐ 7493 9134 0	**Rebuilding Coventry**	Sue Townsend	£5.99

All these books are available at your bookshop or newsagent, or can be ordered direct from the address below. Just tick the titles you want and fill in the form below.

Cash Sales Department, PO Box 5, Rushden, Northants NN10 6YX.
Phone: 01933 414000 : Fax: 01933 414047.

Please send cheque, payable to 'Reed Book Services Ltd.', or postal order for purchase price quoted and allow the following for postage and packing:

£1.00 for the first book, 50p for the second; **FREE POSTAGE AND PACKING FOR THREE BOOKS OR MORE PER ORDER.**

NAME (Block letters) ....

ADDRESS ....

....

☐ I enclose my remittance for ....

☐ I wish to pay by Access/Visa Card Number ☐☐☐☐☐☐☐☐☐☐☐☐☐☐☐☐

Expiry Date ☐☐☐☐

Signature ....

Please quote our reference: MAND